PRAISE FOR
GÖTZ AND MEYER

"*Götz and Meyer* is an astonishing feat. It is a novel in which craft and content are inextricably woven, in which the telling and the told could be no other way." —*The San Diego Union-Tribune*

"[Albahari] has written an impressive commentary on the banality of evil. Highly recommended."
—*Library Journal*

"Decades later, the Holocaust continues to enslave and inspire the European literary imagination—seldom more memorably than in Albahari's brilliantly disturbing novel." —*Kirkus Reviews* (starred review)

"[A] stirring novel ... Readers will be drawn into the professor's obsessive first-person narrative in which the horror is in the facts of bureaucratic efficiency and the unimaginable evil in ordinary life."
—*Booklist*

"Through his narrator's fevered imaginings, Albahari fleshes out the two Nazi officers. Call it the Rosencrantz and Guildenstern approach to history—darkly comic, though without Tom Stoppard's antic absurdity."

—Tess Lewis, WBUR (Boston)

"An extraordinary and gravely moving novel . . . The author's achievement is not just to present the known facts, but to reconstruct and reorder them with an imaginative sympathy that provides a degree of dignity for the victims."

—*The Times Literary Supplement* (London)

"Feels as if it was written by a Serbian Kafka. . . . This is a heartbreaking short book, sardonic and brutal, written at unrelenting pace with great compassion and wild humor."

—*The Independent* (London)

"A harrowing yet very beautiful novel . . . written with a poetic and fastidious precision that reminds me of [Albahari's] late near-contemporary, the great WG Sebald."   —*Literary Review* (London)

"Many powerful books have been written about war—the crimes, the victims, the legacies—and this stark, marvellous work is yet another which revisits the horror, the sadness and the anger while also offering a fresh eloquence, a new profundity and a rare sense of what it is to be human."

—*The Irish Times* (Dublin)

"*Götz and Meyer* is above all a testament to the power of the imagination, which persists relentlessly . . . unable to transform anything but still attempting to grasp the meaningless tragedies of history."

—*The Daily Telegraph* (London)

"In a seamless interplay of historical fact and imagined fiction, gracefully revealed in the growing madness of his protagonist, Albahari shows an aspect of the Holocaust that few writers have yet revealed."

—*Calgary Herald* (Canada)

"The book reads so beautifully and effortlessly that, in light of the subject matter, the reader almost has a guilty conscience. But then without this lyricism the horror of the narrator's experience could hardly be endured."

—*Süeddeutsche Zeitung* (Germany)

GÖTZ AND MEYER

David Albahari

GÖTZ AND MEYER

Translated from the Serbian by
Ellen Elias-Bursać

A Harvest Book
HARCOURT, INC.
Orlando Austin New York San Diego Toronto London

Requests for permission to make copies
of any part of the work should be submitted online at
www.harcourt.com/contact or mailed to the following address:
Permissions Department, Harcourt, Inc., 6277 Sea Harbor Drive,
Orlando, Florida 32887-6777.

www.HarcourtBooks.com

Originally published with the title *Götz i Majer*
by Stubovi kulture, Belgrade, 1998

First published in English in Great Britain in 2004
by the Harvill Press, Random House

The Library of Congress has cataloged
the hardcover edition as follows:
Albahari, David, 1948–
[Gec i Majer. English]
Götz and Meyer/David Albahari;
translated from the Serbian by Ellen Elias-Bursać. 1st U.S. ed.
p.   cm.
I. Title.   II. Elias-Bursać, Ellen.
PG1419.1.L335G413   2005
891.8'236—dc22   2005040359
ISBN-13: 978-0-15-101141-4   ISBN-10: 0-15-101141-9
ISBN-13: 978-0-15-603110-3 (pbk.)   ISBN-10: 0-15-603110-8 (pbk.)

Text set in Sabon

Printed in the United States of America

First Harvest edition 2006
A C E G I K J H F D B

GÖTZ AND MEYER

ötz and Meyer. Having never seen them, I can only imagine them. In twosomes like theirs, one is usually taller, the other shorter, but since both were SS noncommissioned officers, it is easy to imagine that both were tall, perhaps the same height. I am assuming that the standards for acceptance into the SS were rigorous, below a certain height you most certainly would not qualify. One of the two, or so witnesses claim, came into the camp, played with the children, picked them up, even gave them chocolates. We need so little to imagine another world, don't we? But Götz, or Meyer, then went off to his truck and got ready for another trip. The distances were not long, but Götz, or Meyer, was looking forward to the breeze that would play through the open truck window. As he walked toward the truck, the children returned, radiant, to their mothers. Götz and Meyer were probably not novices at the job. Though the assignment was not a big one – we are talking of no more than five thousand souls – the efficiency required meant that only trusted colleagues could handle it. It is entirely possible that Götz and Meyer wore decorations of some sort on their noncommissioned officers' lapels. I wouldn't be surprised. I'd be more surprised if one of them had a mustache. I cannot picture Götz, or Meyer, with facial hair. In fact, I cannot picture them at all. The mustaches are no help. It is simplest, of course, to fall back on stereotypes – blond hair, fair complexion, pale face, and steely eyes – but I would only be demonstrating my vulnerability to propaganda. The chosen race had barely got off the ground, Götz and Meyer represented only one link in a chain stretching far into the future. But what a link they were! Sometimes it is precisely the little tasks such as theirs that form the cornerstone of a vast edifice; their sturdiness ensures the stability of the foundations. I am not saying that Götz and Meyer dwelled on this – perhaps they merely did their job conscientiously as they might have done any other – but they did, undoubtedly, know what their work was for. Their job, more precisely, that was how they referred to it, their assignment, their order, their command. Military terminology cannot be avoided here. Götz and Meyer were, after all, members of the army, one cannot doubt their loyalty to the Reich and the Führer. Even as they came into the camp, swung children up off the ground, Götz, or maybe it was Meyer, never thought for a moment of what was to come. Everything fitted, after all, into a larger plan, each individual has his own destiny, no one, least of all Götz, or Meyer, could change that. He was with the children, therefore, only while he was with them. As soon as he'd ruffled the last tousled head, given out the last piece of candy, lowered the last pair of little feet onto solid ground, they faded from his thoughts and he retreated into his fantasies. Götz, or Meyer, had always wanted to be a fighter pilot. I have no proof whatsoever that this was what he dreamed of, but I find the thought appealing that he'd step up into the cab of his truck as if sliding into the cockpit of a bomber, wearing a leather jacket, but not a pilot's cap because that would have been a little awkward with his fellow traveler sitting there. The truck was a Saurer, a five-tonner with a boxlike body, 1.7 meters high and 5.8 meters long, and it could be hermetically sealed. At first, the Gestapo used smaller trucks, but the Belgrade Saurer was part of a second series, a more perfect series: a full hundred people could stand in the back, apparently, according to what witnesses tell us. One can run a simple calculation based on that and conclude that it was essential for the transport of five thousand souls to make at least fifty trips. During these trips, the souls became real souls, no longer human in form. Götz and Meyer most certainly knew what was happening in the back of the truck, but they definitely would never have described it like that. After all, the people they were driving had no souls, that, at least, was a commonly known fact! Jews were nothing more than mildew on the face of the world! And so, day in and day out, they repeat their practiced routine. First Götz, or Meyer, would drive the truck to the gateway of the camp, and then Meyer, or Götz, would open its capacious back. Orderly and calm, the prisoners would climb up into the truck: women, children, a few of the elderly. Beforehand they would place their belongings in another truck, parked within the confines of the camp. They were convinced that the moment had finally come for them to be transported to Romania, though there had been talk of Poland, as if that mattered, what mattered was that they were leaving this gruesome place, no matter where they went from here it couldn't be worse, and a flash of relief would have crossed their faces. I don't know where Götz and Meyer were at those moments. It is entirely possible that they were sitting in the truck, or maybe there were administrative chores to do, the signing of orders, the filling out of forms. Whatever the case, when they finally got under way – a guard, a German, would come over, take the paperwork from them, confirm that the loading was finished – when they got under way, everything proceeded according to a precise schedule. And it could be no other way, since the bridge spanning the Sava River had been damaged and traffic was crossing it in alternating directions, using just one lane. The truck had to get there at precisely the moment when the Belgrade lane opened. They'd cross the border without stopping, they had a special permit and special plates, and the camp commander would escort them in a special car. Once they'd crossed the bridge and covered a little distance, they'd pull over, and Götz, or Meyer, would get out, crawl under the Saurer, and hook the exhaust pipe up to an opening on the underside of the truck. After that, Götz and Meyer no longer had anything to do but drive, of course. The truck with the belongings had left them behind long before. The souls in the back of the truck had not. They would fly off all at once, precisely when the truck arrived at its destination. The door at the back would open, the corpses would tumble out, the German soldiers would look away, and Serbian prisoners would start the unloading. This was a group of seven prisoners who had been specially selected for the work. The story was that there had been five of them, but since the job turned out to be pretty strenuous – they had to lug the corpses out and bury them in a grave in no time flat – seven is a more likely number. At first they used to take care with the corpses – this was a dead person after all, an asphyxiated woman, a convulsed little child – but then they got to the point where they grabbed each one they came to, there wasn't time to be respectful, not when there were so many, and each one was heavier than any living being would have been. Death is heavy. Death is a weight. Another group of prisoners had dug the grave, though the first seven never saw the others, the graves were already ready before they got there, which was, at least, some sort of consolation. What were Götz and Meyer up to at this point? I expect they were chatting with the camp commander, one of them was certainly smoking, and there was the business of crawling back under the truck and reattaching the exhaust pipe. Little by little, the day would pass. There was always something to do. Götz and Meyer took their seats in the cab, the camp commander got into his car, the four German guards drove the seven Serbian prisoners off in their vehicle. Behind them, the freshly filled grave was still, but by the next day the soil would start buckling, the gases would cause blisters of earth to bulge. There was no avoiding it, Götz and Meyer might have thought, every job has its downside. They drove slowly, there was no hurry. Later, in the evening, one of them would read a book, while the other went for a stroll. You could say that they felt no aftereffects from their everyday duties, no pressures from horrible scenes, they suffered no discomfort from nightmares. They were in fine shape, had a good appetite, there was no residue of disturbing thoughts, not even nostalgia for their homeland. They were, in fact, the best proof of how advances in technology enhance the stability of the human personality. They were living proof that Reichsführer Himmler had been right when he claimed that a more humane form of killing might ease the psychological burden felt by those members of the task forces assigned to shooting Russians and Jews. Here, Götz and Meyer felt no burden at all. Himmler would, I'm sure, have been delighted had he met them. Apparently in August 1941 somewhere near Minsk he was present at a large-scale execution before a firing squad. When he peered into the grave and saw that several of the victims were still alive, and that they were twitching and moaning, he was nauseated. I have no idea whether he vomited and stained his trim uniform, but going pale, knees knocking, was highly improper for a German officer. So when he got back to Berlin, he issued an order to all the services to work out a method of killing that might boost the morale of both the victims and the soldiers assigned to the executions. All the challenges inherent in such a task were met within fewer than four months, and after successful trial runs with Soviet prisoners of war in Sachsenhausen, by the spring of 1942 they had completed the production of thirty special trucks, twenty large ones like our Saurer, and ten smaller ones, Diamonds or Opelblitzes. This truck, one should note, had its predecessor in a hermetically sealed vehicle used as part of the euthanasia program for the mentally ill, in which the victims were put to death with pure carbon monoxide. The brilliant innovation that made Himmler's idea a reality, and that was, after all, key to the further advancement of mass-murder technology, consisted of using engine exhaust instead of carbon monoxide from steel canisters, not only making the whole procedure considerably less costly but also enhancing the impression that the interior of the truck was completely innocent: it looked like the *genuine* interior of a *genuine* truck, which certainly had a salu-tary effect on the victims. It was difficult, I admit, to resist such attention to detail. It did turn out, however, that things were not as simple as that, regardless of the improvement to the victims' spiritual state, because the members of the task forces found that unloading asphyxiated people actually provoked greater psychological discomfort than ordinary firing-squad executions did. At the camp where Götz and Meyer worked, this problem was resolved by engaging the efforts of the seven, or possibly five, Serbian prisoners. They were the ones who dragged out the dead, lined them up in the graves, and buried them. Once they had finished filling the last of the graves, they were shot. I believe that Götz and Meyer saw this, though it is also entirely possible that before this happened they had already set out, following the commander's car, for the Fairgrounds camp, which was emptying. There were always bureaucratic details to be seen to. This happened, as the documents tell us, on May 10, 1942. A month later, the Saurer was on its way back to Berlin. Götz and Meyer went with it. Its rear axle had broken, so it was transported by train. Götz and Meyer most certainly had their own compartment. Those four German policemen had a special compartment, they had earned an extra week of leave, so why not Götz and Meyer? There is nothing to suggest what led to the broken axle, nor is it known why the truck stayed on in Belgrade, unused, for a month when, at least we know this much, its services were sorely needed elsewhere. It is also not at all clear why that axle, if it had to go and break, hadn't snapped long before, thereby slowing the inevitable pace of the suffering. God was not doing much at this juncture for his chosen people. Perhaps he was busy in some other corner of the world, or perhaps he wanted to let the people know they weren't so chosen after all? If a person can't trust the gods, how can he trust other people? The children, for instance, trusted Götz, or was it Meyer, when he strode briskly into the camp, warmed by the spring sun, picked them up and gave them candy. How Götz, or was it Meyer, loved children! It would be hard to find the right words to describe the warmth he felt when his hands rested on those tousled little heads. He gave no thought to lice at moments like that, although he could often spot them crawling in the closely cropped hair. Should I assume, therefore, that Götz, or was it Meyer, was married? Did he have a wife, perhaps children, somewhere in Germany or, maybe, Austria? The other one, the one who did not venture into the camp, probably wasn't married. Love for children doesn't come from heaven – God was not there anyway – rather, it's something you learn, like everything else. Although, I must admit, there is no harm in thinking that he, the other one, in fact refused to pretend. He was there on a certain assignment, and nothing but that job existed for him. While the other fellow was in the camp, he was seeing to administrative work or sitting in the truck with his foot on the accelerator, waiting. Maybe he smoked. He probably smoked. Everyone smoked back then. As far as that is concerned, the world hasn't changed. Cigarettes have got thinner, filters have reached design perfection, tobacco has become more aromatic, but nothing in them evokes the flood that, at the time of this story, had enveloped the world like slippery slime. Flood, perhaps, is not the best word to use when speaking of people dying from poison gas, but the sensation of submersion is the same. You reach bottom, and that is the end, there is nowhere left to go. Death is not a balloon but an anchor. The souls, indeed, flew up when the truck arrived at its destination, frantic for fresh air, but the bodies stayed below, sometimes so tangled that the Serbian prisoners cursed softly through their clenched teeth as they did what they could to disentangle the arms and legs and crisscrossed fingers. They'd been promised, I read this somewhere, that after they'd completed the job successfully they'd be sent off to a work camp in Norway, and so they lived for two months within a delusion that was part and parcel of the greater delusion, a performance in which each played the role he had been assigned. No improvisation was permitted. All of it, even art, served the stated goal. If each of them had acted according to his own free will, the whole thing would have crumbled early on. The camp prisoners pretended that they were on their way to Romania, or Poland, and climbed into the truck as if they were marching off to no-man's-land between barbed-wire borders. The Serbian prisoners, mud-splattered, plunged their shovels into the soil and sprinkled it on the overflowing graves as if they were building a bridge spanning the North Sea. And just as the truck was not, in fact, headed for Romania, or Poland for that matter, the bridge they were building took them nowhere. During a flood, there is no dry land. Who could have known? Life is full of tricks, anyway, in war and in peace, it makes no difference. It is always that same convulsive effort to survive just a little longer than planned. Present or absent, God is cruel, there is no genuine mercy in him. When he blinks, he blinks, and there is absolutely nothing to be done about it. Souls cluster around him, voices waft his way like the sound of a thousand little bells, but God merely shrugs them off. That was precisely Götz's, or was it Meyer's, shrug of vexation when he saw the broken axle. Something like that must infuriate a person, even if he is as disciplined as Götz and Meyer were. Some things are simply stronger than all that the human spirit creates. And besides, Götz, or was it Meyer, or both, had had it with that wild country, the crude people, the lack of order. It isn't that Götz, or was it Meyer, was nostalgic, his sense of duty was far greater than any homesickness he might have felt, but it was nice, it had to be said, in the quiet of his room, to eat sausages and drink beer. Had he had supernatural powers at his command, Götz, or Meyer, would have fixed that axle with his own hands and returned it to its original condition. Other trucks in the series had indeed been damaged, especially on the rough roads in Russia and Ukraine, but this was no consolation for Götz, or Meyer, or both of them. A person gets accustomed to things and starts expecting the things to accustom themselves to him with the same ease, and when those things betray him, he is rightly disappointed. Not so much so, at least in the case of Götz and Meyer, that he might kick them, here I am referring to the truck, or say something nasty. And not just because the truck had served them well, but because, unlike the people it transported, it had a soul. Götz, or was it Meyer, knew it did, because countless times, while he had been driving, he had felt the cab envelop him in a maternal sort of way. It did all it could to ease his every movement. If the truck had been able to, Götz, or Meyer, was convinced, it would have flown. It only took two days in Berlin to repair the damage, and, as of June 15, 1942, the truck was on its way to Riga. I do not know whether Götz and Meyer were dispatched along with it. If they were not, it is difficult to comprehend the vastness of their grief. They had cleaned it and polished it so often, wiped down the headlights, washed the windshield and the interior! A tougher man than Götz and Meyer might find tears welling up in his eyes at the thought. In fact, that first night after they were faced with the horror of the broken axle, Götz, or was it Meyer, did, indeed, feel despair as he lay in bed. There can be no talk, here, of tears, but something clutched in his chest, pressure from within him and from without, he could barely breathe. He stretched his arms and crossed them under his head, but that didn't help. There was no light in the room, and he could see the sky through the window, sprinkled with stars. Their flickering said something to him, he couldn't grasp what they were saying, but he felt that the message was somehow related to the discomfort he felt, which was not letting up. Was this the cosmic pain he had read about somewhere? Poor Götz, or was it Meyer. I would have liked to have seen his photograph, perhaps then I could describe the expression on his face. I never saw them, Götz or Meyer, so I can only imagine them. My interest in the two of them came at a time when I was trying to fill in the empty slots in my family tree. I had just turned fifty, I knew where I was going with my life, so all that was left was to figure out where I had come from. I went round the archives, visited museums, brought books home from the library. That is how Götz and Meyer came into my life. Almost all the women from my father's and mother's families died, as people usually put it, at the Fairgrounds camp, though in fact they died on the streets and byways of Belgrade, in the truck Götz and Meyer drove out to the execution grounds in Jajinci. Those two names are first mentioned in a telegram from SS-Obergrupenführer Heinrich Müller, head of the Berlin Gestapo, sent in mid-March 1942, to the chief of the German police in Belgrade, SS-Standartenführer Emanuel Schäfer. The telegram announces the arrival of the specialists with the special-purpose truck, and that they will present their orders upon arrival. I have to confess that this drew me to Götz and Meyer, the fact that they were not little cogs in a vast mechanism, blissfully unaware of what the mechanism was for, rather they were entirely aware of the nature of their assignment, being simultaneously the heralds of death and death itself. I tried to picture the moment when their superior officer informed them of the purpose of their journey. Götz and Meyer are standing at ease, barking their Yes, Sirs, but maybe they didn't even need an explanation, maybe they had already gained enough experience on the Eastern Front, this is plausible enough, especially if you consider the requirement for maximum efficiency. In that sense, the staff must be so smoothly rehearsed that they would present no risk or weak link in the chain, so Götz and Meyer could hardly have been novices. I tried to picture how, if they were married men, they had said good-bye to their wives. Götz, or maybe Meyer, would kneel before his wife and rest his cheek on her stomach, while Meyer, or maybe Götz, would plant a kiss on his wife's head. What did he say to her? How much did his wife know? She must have known something, those things slip out, perhaps one of the men talked in his sleep, or maybe he blurted something out during dinner. But, in times of war, it is best, if you are not a direct participant, to know as little as possible, because this is at least a tiny victory over a reality that is the same for everyone, regardless of political conviction. No matter how strange it may sound, it is sometimes easier to understand women than men. What, for instance, did Götz, and Meyer, talk about as they drove to Belgrade? I doubt that they admired the beauty of the flat or hilly landscape, though Götz, or was it Meyer, would quote a verse from Goethe from time to time. They did not speak of the job either, which had already become routine by then, or the calculation, which showed how many days were left until they could go home. (Fifty-four by their count, in fact around eighty.) They may have talked about their return, but then what else would they have to talk about during all the days that stretched before them in that godforsaken hole? Götz, or was it Meyer, the one who was married, was anxious about his daughter Hilda's frequent sore throats. She'll grow out of them, Meyer, or was it Götz, consoled him, the one who was probably not married, but it is true, he added, that one must attend to one's health from childhood. As a boy, for instance, he had longed to be a pilot, but he had not looked after himself, and if he had done a better job, he would have made a better showing on the tests and examinations, and right now, why, he might have been sitting in the cockpit of a Messerschmitt. Götz, or maybe Meyer, had quite a laugh over that story! He slapped his knee. Applauded. But Meyer, or maybe Götz, meant it. His leather pilot's jacket hung in the cab, and from time to time he'd put it on, with his fellow traveler's silent consent. Then he liked to open the window and feel the wind in his face. At first he was distracted from his fantasies by the dull thumps and muted cries audible from the back of the truck, but as time passed he no longer noticed them. A person can get used to anything, why not that? And the thumping never lasted long, or the cries, because most of them in there were women and children. It all took longer with grown men, even the thumping, so, at least as far as that was concerned, their work was easier. Götz and Meyer must have known, how could they not, that almost all the Jewish men in Serbia had already been shot. How this had happened they didn't know, or how the operation had been organized, but, truth be told, they didn't care. I, however, did know how it happened: almost all the men in my mother's and father's families were killed in the autumn of 1941. Assembled earlier in various collection camps and jails, they were taken off to be shot in smaller and larger groups, often in retaliation for German soldiers who had been killed. Buried at various execution grounds around Belgrade, they created a tangled web of death that I never managed to disentangle completely. As for the ones at the Fairgrounds, at least we know the precise route: over the Sava River bridge, through Belgrade, to Jajinci. I know the route; they didn't. While they were in the line behind the truck, they believed that they were headed for a new camp in Romania, or maybe Poland. Hadn't that been what the camp commander told them, a man named Andorfer who had even made the effort to produce rules for the new camp and distribute them to the members of the Jewish Administration? Quite by chance, though maybe not, Untersturmführer Andorfer, before he dedicated himself professionally to the SS, worked as the business manager of a hotel. The conditions for accommodation in that hotel in Sölden am Öztal were far better than they were at the Fairgrounds camp, where broken windows were boarded up, cracks yawned in the walls, and the roofs leaked. No wonder, then, that, at first, the prisoners in the camp volunteered for the transport: to get as far away from that hellhole as possible. They were humiliated not only by the camp's subhuman conditions but by its full exposure to Belgrade, which watched them from across the river. The pain is more acute when what has been lost hovers constantly before your eyes. Silence can kill. Order is essential in all things, thought Götz and Meyer as they checked in with Standartenführer Emanuel Schäfer, head of the

German police, otherwise a doctor of law. Schäfer informed Camp Commander Andorfer of everything, and he, in turn, told everything to his deputy, Edgar Enge. Before the war, or rather up to the moment he was drafted, Enge had worked as a tour guide. So it was that the operation for the final solution of the Jewish question in Serbia was, in fact, put into practice by a former hotelier and a former tour guide, quite ironic though hardly absurd if one keeps in mind the affinities between the two lines of work, using the same vocabulary: accommodation, transport, daily and weekly menus, the ordering of food supplies, hygiene, guests' complaints. Perhaps one cannot speak of the camp prisoners as guests, perhaps one shouldn't, and their complaints were hardly taken seriously. In formal terms, the German occupying forces were the host, but the purchasing of food was financed from funds acquired by selling looted Jewish property. The camp prisoners paid for their own accommodation. A total of 26,900,000 dinars was paid to the Municipality of Belgrade for food, the caloric value of which contributed to the great speed with which the prisoners lost weight, ultimately making Götz and Meyer's job all the easier. The German occupying forces demonstrated the same efficiency when, in mid-October 1941, they decided to shoot the remaining four thousand Jewish men, excepting from that number approximately three hundred, whom they designated to maintain order among the women, children, and elderly people in the Jewish ghetto, which was supposed to be in the "Gypsy Quarter" of Belgrade but which was never built. Instead of a ghetto, they opened the Fairgrounds camp. Here their efficiency came to the fore once more: they used pavilions that had since 1937 been the site of international fairs. So the Turkish Pavilion was, with startling aptness, where they set up the baths and, later, the mortuary. The connection between a bath and a mortuary is not entirely obvious, unless one sees the act of death, no matter how ugly it may be, as a transition to a state of greater purity. The camp-command quarters settled into a little building near the gate that used to house the Fairgrounds administration. The Jewish Administration of the camp was located at the Central Tower. Most of the prisoners lived in the third pavilion, the largest of them all, where all the partitions had been torn down. The surface area of this pavilion was about five thousand square meters, which means that each person, and as many as five thousand souls were there, had the living space of a single square meter. The mortality rate was rather high among the prisoners even before

Götz and Meyer got to Belgrade, so sometimes they had more space, which the prisoners mostly weren't aware of, and therefore they weren't able to make use of it. One shouldn't hold that against the prisoners, because they were glad if they could move about at all. That was precisely why they were so delighted when Götz, Meyer, and their truck appeared at the gate to the camp: if nothing else, they'd be going somewhere where there would be more food and where they could stretch their legs properly. At such moments life is measured in small increments: the length of one's bed, for instance, or woolen socks. It was certainly no better at the first pavilion where the Jews brought in later were accommodated, although I don't know precisely how large a surface area it covered. A kitchen was later opened in the fourth pavilion; at first, food was delivered by car from Belgrade. The Jewish men, the ones who were spared execution by firing squad, lived in the fifth pavilion. The second pavilion was set aside for Gypsies, and afterward they made camp workshops there: a locksmith's, cobbler's, tailor's, and carpenter's shop. The camp had its own hospital and pharmacy: fifty cots or so at the pavilion of the Nikola Spasić Foundation. A real little city unto itself, make no mistake Such a shame they had to squat out in the open to relieve themselves; if there had been some tidier solution for this, the Fairgrounds might have become a model Nazi camp. This made Commander Andorfer even more unhappy. He was a young man, in his thirties, brimming with energy, thrilled to be alive in the triumphal time of the German Reich, and if there was a war going on around him, and there was, he wanted to be part of it. His petitions were not heard, and he remained in this position until late April 1942, when the Jewish question in Serbia was almost completely solved, and Götz, and Meyer, began having dreams about going home. Götz, in particular, or maybe it was Meyer, had vivid dreams, so much so that he woke up at night, in a sweat if he had dreamed something unpleasant, radiant if he had stepped, in his dream, into his childhood home. Sometimes he wouldn't wake up at all but would howl and tremble, and Meyer, unless it was Götz, had to get up, shake him, and squeeze his shoulders. You could hear similar screams in the third pavilion at night, although they were more often caused by water or urine pouring down between the boards of the bunk beds than they were by nightmares. Reality was bad enough, there was no need to dream something else, at least not at night. By day you were lucky to be dreaming, because the conviction that everything was happening to you as if in a dream, to someone else, helped you get through the time from dawn to dusk. I am speaking as if time were a river, as if it were the Sava flowing by them, but they wouldn't have had the strength to wade across even a little stream. They crossed the Sava only in the truck driven by Götz and Meyer, or shrouded in white sheets, stiff and dead, on stretchers carried by Jewish men across the frozen river, the ones who had been kept from the firing squad, and the Jewish women who hadn't died yet. So the camp prisoners not only fed themselves, they tended their dead themselves. And Götz and Meyer might say that they even killed themselves, because they breathed poisonous fumes without being forced to, and the more they inhaled, the more, paradoxically, they exhaled of their own lives. Sounds absurd, I know, and, chances are, this never occurred to Götz and Meyer, but this was a way they could shrug off responsibility and pile it on the shoulders of other people. Once you become part of the mechanism, you assume the same responsibility as every other part. Götz and Meyer didn't know about that. The truck was theirs to drive, and they drove, always smiling, even when the wind blew dust in their faces, and they couldn't care less what was going on in the back, whether the load was Jews or sugar beets. When the door at the back opens, the suffocated bodies tumble out, the first of them thuds to the ground, the others pile out on top of them with softer and softer thuds, until finally the last corpses slip out onto the others in total silence. Unprepared for this, surrounded by four German sentries, the five Serbian prisoners, or was it seven, step back in the face of this avalanche of the dead, but the grasping, stiffened Jewish hands brush their clogs. And where were Götz and Meyer at that moment? What was Andorfer doing? Was he supervising the unloading, or had he stepped back, shifting impatiently from one foot to the other, or chewing, perhaps, on a dry blade of grass? When I first tried to sketch out my family tree, it looked like that blade of grass, like a bare tree, without leaves. I gleaned a few names from a senile old relative of mine who was spending his final days in an old people's home up on Bežanijska Kosa. I enticed him with chocolates, which he was not allowed to eat because he had diabetes, and so it was that, for a moment, I pulled aside the curtain of his memory loss. At that point I didn't know that Götz, or was it Meyer, had also used chocolates as a form of deceit, though in his case the candy served to close the curtain of memory loss rather than open it, which, I have to say, is a big difference. A curtain is a curtain, no doubt, but life does not proceed in nouns, life proceeds in verbs. I read somewhere that the Serbian prisoners did their job in less than an hour that first day, to the unconcealed delight of Commander Andorfer, who felt that the smooth functioning of the staff and the unquestionable efficiency of the effort were a marvelous sign: the special assignment, as he put it in his telegram to the Gestapo, was under way, and now all they had to do was finish it, and after that Andorfer's dream of a transfer closer to the front lines would come true, and he would be able to join in the struggle against the evil Communists. Andorfer, however, found the camp itself to be a bit unpleasant, because he had got to know, over time, the members of the Jewish Administration, and he even played cards and drank coffee with some of them. I don't know whether what they drank was genuine or ersatz coffee, and I did not manage to establish what it was they played: tablonet or, perhaps, rummy, or some other game meant to pass the time. My cousin, for instance, played solitaire. He had big, fleshy ears, a drooping lower lip, and watery eyes. Despite my best intentions, I could recognize nothing of myself in him. When I put that first chocolate on the table, he reached out, squeezed it, brought it to his nose, then stuffed it in his mouth and mumbled, "Klara." A thin droplet of chocolate drool slipped down his chin. After the second chocolate, he said, "Flora." After the third, he asked me if I'd shave him. I demanded to hear another name first. I held my pencil, there was a piece of paper before me on the table, I was ready to write. "Matilda," my cousin said, "Bukica, Estera, Sara, Mara, Lenka, Rašela, Rifka, Zlata." I hurriedly wrote down the names, the pencil flew across the paper, I hoped that I would be able to read them later. The cousin fell silent. I took out another chocolate, asking him for men's names. "David," said my cousin and closed his eyes, "Isak, Daniel, Bata, Jakov, Moric, Leon, Samuilo, Ruben, Rafael, Haim, Solomon, Ilija, Josif, Marko, Moša, Avram." Then I shaved him. Götz and Meyer were always freshly shaven, especially the one who came into the camp and picked up the children, because he knew that children were afraid of beards, unless it was a long, white beard like the one Father Christmas had. I doubt the boys and girls who came over to him knew who Father Christmas was, and I am certain that they wouldn't have been put off by a bristly beard on the face of a man who came in and out of their lives like an angel, leaving them gifts. Their mothers didn't stop them. After all, Götz and Meyer looked a little like angels to them, too, since their arrival heralded the long-awaited departure. And who else but an angel would be spiriting them away from such a place, who else could have heard their anguish? I went to my cousin's room three or four more times, always with a paper bag of chocolates in my pocket, and I managed to squeeze out a few more first and last names, to establish the lines of marriage and the closeness of kinship, and to determine, at least roughly, the number of male and female descendants. Then, as I wiped the bits of chocolate and bubbles of drool from his face, I decided I'd end the masquerade, because if I were to continue, it occurred to me, I would most certainly be hastening his end, which would make me no better than Götz, or Meyer, regardless of the fact that at the time I hadn't heard of him, or rather, them. My family tree now looked quite different, it had filled out with leaves and branches, and it was sturdier. Judging by the image it projected, I ought to have had sixty-seven relatives, some of them close, others more distant, while, as I later discovered, in fact I had only six, including the cousin in the old people's home up on Bežanijska Kosa. Actually: only five, because my cousin died shortly thereafter, in his pajamas, in bed, asleep. Every death should happen in one's sleep, easy and painless, the way the good Lord meant it to be, I said to myself as the rabbi sang over his grave. I hoped that mine, too, would be like that. I started to search, to tour dusty archives and visit museums, I brought home new books from the library, stared at group photographs, compared various reports, compared lists. I buried myself in the lives of others, as if they were mine, which they were, in fact, though my life didn't know that. I was an ear of corn with nothing but a few loose kernels left on it. One of them, I learned later, was an aunt in Argentina, another stood for a cousin who lived in Israel, a third was a distant relation in America, and the fourth and fifth cousins were off at the edge of the ear of corn, instead of Grandpa's youngest brother and an even younger sister who were now living, as an old man and woman, in Australia. I had never married. In other words, when all of us died off, when our kernels fell into the washtub of time, nothing would be left from my parents' families. At first, this realization stirred a fierce rebellion within me; then I calmed down. You don't get anywhere with anger, it is only poison coursing through your veins, blurring your reason, and nothing could alter the fact that I was a wrinkled apple at the end of a dry branch on a with-ered tree. You can't cure yourself of death. I would be willing to bet that Götz and Meyer never so much as thought of such a thing. At their age, and I am prepared to believe that they were younger than Commander Andorfer, you don't often think about death, at least not your own, not even when you are in a war. They had all their teeth; their hair, though short, was still thick, their skin taut, their muscles toned, their hearts healthy. Who would be thinking of death, especially at the wheel of a powerful Saurer truck? And powerful it most certainly was, because its strength was measured not in tons or kilometers, but in human souls. From the Fairgrounds to the foot of the Avala Hills it swallowed up eighty souls like a breeze, sometimes a full hundred, and all the while it never tired, there'd be no trace of overheating or exhaustion. Not even on those days when the truck traveled the same route twice, bringing the sum of transported souls dangerously close to a total of two hundred, with not a trace to be seen on the truck. "This is one fine truck," Götz and Meyer would say, "loyal as a horse, tough as a donkey and stubborn as a mule." There were no better words to describe that technical wonder, to sum up its inner and outer features so precisely. The prisoners, no doubt, though this has not been recorded anywhere, experienced it quite differently: like a carriage or a magic carpet to transport them high, high above the earth, and then lower them gently back down to reality. They didn't know just how close to the truth they were. That, of course, is my own fabrication, which I came to later, after I'd reconstructed their lives and tried to decode their deaths. That was also not an easy task, let's not fool ourselves. First I had to establish their names, then I figured out their addresses and occupations, their membership in various organizations, religious and secular, their political leanings, their involvement in administrative and supervisory boards, the schools they attended, the excursions they went on, the property they owned. I bought a map of Belgrade and marked where they had lived with "x"s. I don't know what I expected from this, but the little "x"s did not, in their random pattern, spell out any sort of secret message for me. The city had changed in the meantime, and some of the little "x"s were now in the middle of squares or parks, in playing fields or beneath new high-rises. Some houses, especially in the Dorćol neighborhood, were still standing, most often with crumbling facades, dented gutters, and damp hallways. I went there, stood in front of them, and watched, as if they had something they could tell me, and I'd poke around until I started noticing worried faces behind the curtains. I got so heavy with all the lives, with the shadows of these lives, that sometimes I could barely get myself to move. Götz, and Meyer, would most certainly have criticized me for this. Both of them were slender, and both were ready, as soon as they got up in the morning, still in their underwear, for physical exercise. Furthermore, Götz, although it might have been Meyer, regularly ate fresh fruit, but he was also fond of stewed apples and had a particular weakness for prunes. Once, for instance, they talked for a long time about the importance of prunes for regular digestion, and another time Götz, or was it Meyer, the one who was not, perhaps, married, pointed out to Meyer, or was it Götz, the one who probably was, that fresh fruit, if you had enough of it, was just the sort of thing to ease his little daughter's frequent sore throats. Meyer, or was it Götz, was always anxious about that, and he'd ask his wife in every letter home to take good care of their little girl and to write to him about how the girl was faring. You get a sore throat today, tomorrow it's pneumonia, and the day after it's anybody's guess. A person must remain vigilant, therein lies the art of living. One day you relax your standards, and the next day you are in a camp, so it goes. Jews, this much they knew in the Reich, had been physically unprepared, they dedicated all their attention to spiritual achievements and to mumbling prayers, as if the spirit and prayers could shield them from everything, and as soon as they were faced with physical trouble, they'd snuff out like candles in the wind. Until the spring of 1941, more precisely: until April 16, the members of my father's and mother's families lived to an average age, some of them even reaching a ripe, old age, but between then and May 1942, the percentage of their mortality rises steeply, and their lives get shorter and shorter. All that was left of a healthy family tree was a clipped crown with the occasional rickety branch. I stared at those two years that had gnawed away at the leaves of my tree like caterpillars. I had to press my fists to my chest, my heart pounded so. And Götz, or was it Meyer, once clutched at his heart, but that was when the axle broke on the Saurer. It was my life breaking, that was the difference. You can always weld an axle, and later it will, as they say, be good as new, but once a life breaks, it is broken forever. Wherever you turn, you trip up, no repairs can make it better. In other circumstances, I could have gone to see a doctor and said: Doctor, my heart is broken. Had I been the doctor, I would have chuckled. Instead, I wandered the streets of Belgrade searching for ghosts. From the outside, I looked like an old pensioner trudging down the street, my shoulders hunched, my hands crossed behind my back, but deep inside I was hurrying from place to place, terrified, breathless, feeling myself collapse in the general disarray of my being. No, nothing like that could ever have happened to Götz, and Meyer, even less to Untersturmführer Andorfer or Scharführer Enge. They were the same on the outside and on the inside. Then I still didn't know anything about them. I didn't really know anything at all. My parents, while they were still alive, said nothing about their past: what happened happened, and there was no point in discussing it. When they died, I was drawn to other things: strolling in Kalemegdan Park and, above all else, my collection of stamps with portraits of writers and literary motifs. They never even spoke of their own, or my, Jewish identity, convinced, I guess, that if evil were to come knocking at our door again, the silence would make us invisible. So what I knew was limited to the most general facts from textbooks, history, films, and works of literature, which didn't in any way suggest that those facts had anything to do with me. History was, after all, impersonal, at least as a discipline, it couldn't exist at the level of the individual, because then it would be impossible to grasp. That was why every history came down to searching for the smallest and largest common denominators, as if every person were the same, and all human destinies were equal. Perhaps it might seem that these claims were unfounded, but I will try to explain them with a simple example. History drily informs us that the German occupying forces issued an order on April 16, 1941, to register and identify all Jews, and that by July 13 that same year, as is stated in the periodical business report that the Municipality of Belgrade submitted to the Ministry of the Interior, nearly 9,500 Belgrade Jews registered. This is where history has no more to say. All you need to do, however, is to wonder how each of those 9,500 men, women, and children felt when they donned the yellow armband or the six-pointed star, and history begins to crumble and fail. History has no time for feelings, even less for trauma and pain, and least of all for dull helplessness, for the inability to grasp what is happening. One day you are a human being, and the next, despite the armband or perhaps precisely because of it, you are invisible. No, that is not history, it is a catastrophe of cosmic proportions, in which every individual is a separate cosmos. Nine thousand five hundred universes shift from a steady to a gaseous state, more than merely metaphorically, especially when you think of those five thousand souls who became acquainted with the back of Götz and Meyer's truck. I'll give you an example: an order was issued on May 30 that same year by the military commander in Serbia, according to which all Jews, and with them Gypsies, had to report their property within ten days. The Legal Department was responsible for seeing to this by order of the Municipal Assembly President on June 4, and was, at the same time, responsible for submitting the processed reports to the District Command Office. The Legal Department did its part of the job within the given deadline and, as early as June 14, sent on a list of 3,474 Jews and Gypsies who had reported their property, pointing out in the enclosed letter that the department would not be able to send on the reports to the District Command Office because, among other things, they had no clerk proficient in German, nor had they a single typewriter that could type in anything but Cyrillic. That much is history. Outside history are all those years, knowledge, and skill that each of the people on that list had invested in acquiring their property, whether they were street vendors, chemists, lawyers, or housewives, and outside history remains the impact of the fact that in all those documents the words *Jew* and *Gypsy* were written "jew" and "gypsy," in lowercase. Inferior people cannot command superior letters. Later you could see that at the Fairgrounds camp, too, where everyone, particularly the men, was expected to greet any

German by doffing his cap and bowing to the ground. I could not have done it, not with this spine I've been troubled with for so many years. All it takes is a single, incautious gesture, too great a strain or a sudden twist, and I can barely move for days, stiff as a mast pole, and I spend those nights on the floor or sleeping on a board with only a thin mattress over it. Götz and Meyer, I'm sure, wouldn't have been fazed by this in the least, I mean the hardness of the floor or the board. They were soldiers used to the exigencies of war, and they could drop off to sleep anywhere, in the truck, in a meadow, or in a ditch, although Götz, and Meyer, too, was fondest of sleeping under a feather quilt. First you shiver a little from the coolness of the sheets, then warmth slowly envelops you, and then you dream dreams soft as feathers. If, as you settle into bed, you can see a quince on top of your bureau, and its fragrance gradually fills your nostrils, the experience will be complete. Of course, the women and children at the Fairgrounds camp could only dream of quinces and feather quilts. Although some of them had brought bedding with them, most of them slept on bare boards, here and there spread with a thin layer of straw. In those war years there wasn't much of anything. The same went for straw: there was never enough, which, in the end, suited only the fleas. As soon as I think of fleas, I start to scratch and run my fingers through my hair. Götz, or was it Meyer, the one who gave candy to the children, clearly was not as squeamish as I am. Perhaps at home, in Germany or Austria, he had a dog, so he was used to fleas, was quick to catch them and, with a little crunch, crush them between his fingers. I never saw Götz or Meyer, so I can only imagine them, but somehow I feel certain that Götz, or Meyer, had a poodle, a small fluffy thing called Lily. If Lily had only come to the Fairgrounds camp once, what joy she would have brought those children! They would have crowded round her, touched her little nose, patted her little tail and paws, forgotten all about the chocolates. In a report dated February 6, 1942, sent by Commander Andorfer to the Municipality of Belgrade, there were 1,136 children at the camp who were under sixteen years of age, and seventy-six children still nursing. The total number, clearly, kept changing, new prisoners arrived at the camp until late February, and even later. Among them were about three hundred Jewish women and children from a camp in Niš, while there were certainly children among those dying of disease, cold, and abuse. The dead were laid out in the Turkish Pavilion. Whenever twenty or so corpses were collected, they'd be carried across the frozen Sava, shrouded in white sheets, to the Belgrade shore. In short, according to my calculations, assuming that there were a number of children, mostly somewhat older, among the victims of the firing squads from the time before Götz and Meyer's truck arrived, and continuing, in some instances, in parallel with their activities, it turns out that death, in the back of that truck, sought – though death does not, in fact, seek but simply arrives – at least a thousand children and no fewer than fifty infants. According to another calculation, much more precise and based on counting the branches and twigs on my family tree, among them were about a dozen children from my parents' families between the ages of two and fifteen. Although Götz, or Meyer, did not have as many chocolates as there were children at the camp, I allow myself to presume that at least one of those twelve got hold of one of the tasty dark brown balls that, like a magic spell, at least momentarily made his or her life happier. Happiness, however, melts every bit as fast as chocolate in the mouth, and no matter how much my little cousin tried to keep that taste on his tongue, it melted away, disappeared, and gave way to the vagaries of memory. Memory, no matter how strange this might sound, was the single constant at the Fairgrounds camp, especially at 5:00 in the morning, when the prisoners were awakened by a bugle and then filed out for the inspection conducted by the camp commander or his deputy. At 6:00 A.M. they were given breakfast, at noon, lunch, and at 6:00 P.M., dinner, and at 8:00 all the prisoners had to be in their pavilions, on their cots. An orderly life, no two ways about it, though not what the Belgrade Jews had had in mind, exactly, if they had had anything in mind, when they began to respond to the summonses of the Special Police for Jews. By then, almost all the Jewish men had been shot, so it was women, children, and the elderly who were standing in the long lines in front of the police station. They were permitted to bring with them three days' worth of food, eating utensils, bedding, and as much luggage as they could carry themselves. From there for the next five days they were taken, group by group, over the Sava River to the camp. First they had to lock their apartments and cellars, and surrender their keys marked with legibly written tags indicating their names and addresses. These bundles of keys, jangling cheerfully as they changed hands, were their tickets for transport. You handed them the keys, you took your place in the truck – nothing simpler. Among them, along with those twelve children, again a calculation of mine, there were twenty-three of my relatives, eighteen women and five older people. Only one man, named Haim, whose name was gloriously altered to Benko in certain documents and who, as a doctor, had been kept on duty at the Jewish hospital in Dorćol, was still among the living, not counting, of course, the cousins who I later learned were living abroad, or my father, who, as a reserve second lieutenant of the prewar Yugoslav Army, had been taken into custody at one of the prisoner-of-war camps for officers in Germany. My mother was already hiding, with me, in the Serbian village of S——. She never spoke of it to me. While she was still alive, she refused to talk about the past, and at that point the past didn't interest me either. I learned that detail later, when I immersed myself in the sea of documents and testimony kept at the Jewish Historical Museum in Belgrade. I was one and a half years old when we got to that village, and four and a half when we left, and all I remember are chickens pecking at crumbs from my little palm. My mother was twenty-seven at the time, and my father, thirty-five. They had married in April 1939, and I came into the world on May 18 of the next year, though it might just as well have been May 17, because I was born at midnight. Götz and Meyer did not know this as they drove toward Belgrade. At one moment, during the drive, Götz, or Meyer, burst into lively yodeling to cheer up Meyer, or was it Götz, who was saddened by the thought of his ailing little daughter. Götz, or was it Meyer, despite his yodeling, felt that Meyer, or maybe it was Götz, was a bit too soft for such responsible duties, though he never said as much. Softness is the first step to insecurity, their officers told them time and time again, but the fact that Meyer, or maybe Götz, completed every assignment fully and promptly dissuaded Götz, or maybe Meyer, from his doubts. And so they traveled, the mountains gave way to plains, the forest to plowed fields, the rapids of mountain streams to the phlegmatic, sluggish Danube, and finally they caught sight of Belgrade. The truck chugged along, reliable as ever, and there was every suggestion, including a lovely sunset, that Götz and Meyer would complete the task they had been assigned to everyone's satisfaction. You could count those who were dissatisfied, with the exception of the camp inmates themselves and those five or seven Serbian prisoners, on the fingers of one hand. And as for instances of dissatisfaction with the Saurer truck that drove the Fairgrounds–Jajinci route, that hand might as well have been fingerless: there wasn't a single criticism to count. Commander Andorfer's request, when he asked, right in the middle of the extermination process, to be transferred to a new post closer to the front lines, can be explained by his nose: he could smell, symbolically speaking, the stench of carbon monoxide and felt it was high time to be smelling, instead, the fragrance of gunpowder. These smells are all of them unknown to me. I missed the carbon monoxide by a hair, as people often say, and, thanks to certain health problems I don't intend to go into here, I was freed of my obligation to serve in the army. To tell you the truth, I don't know whether carbon monoxide has much of a recognizable smell, and gunpowder, they say, stinks more than it smells, though that is no excuse for my ignorance. But if you admit you don't know, you always have the edge over those who guess. That was how I consoled myself while I sat there collecting data for my family tree. Only when I had finished it did I realize that I was only at the beginning, that there is no such thing as ultimate knowledge, rather each new step forward in knowing something is a vestibule leading into new realms of ignorance. I wanted to discover who I was and what I was, and where I had come from, and the closer I got, the farther I was from it. I took a city bus down to the Fairgrounds and walked among the crumbling buildings, stared at the ground as if I might find something there, listened to the wind in the trees, hopped carefully over the cracks in the concrete slabs. I didn't find a thing. The windows in the high-rises of New Belgrade gleamed, in front of me Belgrade was outlined against a stormy sky, a void swelled inside me, beneath me murmured the dead. The completed family tree, drawn on a large piece of white paper, lay on the desk in my sitting room. I carefully wrote out all the names and dates, underlined in black marker all the family lines, circled in red all the names of people who were still alive. I started drawing the first version from above, descending in all directions, and then I stopped, thinking that the network of life and death shouldn't look like a fern dangling from a flowerpot suspended from a hook on the ceiling. The next time I started from below, at the spot where the tree should have its roots, and only then was I able to breathe a sigh of relief. Above the dense treetop, my branch protruded like a young shoot stubbornly refusing to admit that the tree had withered. At the age of fifty, especially taking my ailing spine into consideration, I would have been better off speaking of myself as a stick rather than as a young shoot, but therein lies the absurdity of every representation of life, and any representation of reality will never be the same as reality itself, and there is nothing I can do about it. So, I figured, if I couldn't dive into life, perhaps I could dive into death. Hence Götz and Meyer. By the way, Götz was called Wilhelm, and Meyer's name was Erwin. I never saw them and I could only imagine them, as I did from the moment when I first stumbled upon their names, and as I shall do until the moment I close my eyes forever – I have always been appalled at the prospect of dying with my eyes open – and go off to wherever it is that nearly all my relatives went. My life split in an orderly and painless fashion into three parallel lives. One continued to belong only to me: in that life, I got up in the morning, shaved, had breakfast, went to work, came home, unlocked my letter box, read the paper, had lunch and dinner, watched television. My second life was one of constant transformations: in that life, staring at the family tree, which, like some sort of masterpiece, I had framed and hung on the wall, I would become, by turns, one of my vanished cousins: sometimes a woman, sometimes a little girl or boy, or perhaps an old man resting his hand on a prayer book, a merchant's assistant among his bolts of cloth, a baker or a pharmacist. The third life had two heads: I was at once both Götz and Meyer, the angel of death and the driver, a soldier and a simple man, the pretend savior and the real executioner. In such confusion, it is not difficult to imagine that there were moments when I did not know who I was. I would pour myself a glass of water, drink it as Götz, or Meyer, but my throat would still feel parched like little Estera's when the door slammed at the back of the Saurer. In the evening I'd get into bed as my father's brother, and I'd be assaulted by dreams of a village in the Austrian Alps. There were countless such examples, which does not mean, I hope no one will think this, that I was a nutcase. From the outside you wouldn't have noticed a thing: from the inside, if such a thing were possible, you wouldn't have noticed any changes either; it was my same feeble body, my same spineless spirit. It would make more sense to say, if I may allow myself the freedom, that I was holding an enchanted fairy-tale looking glass, and its surface would cloud over from time to time, and suddenly you could see a woman's smooth countenance or a man's grimace in it. In short, I was the reflection of other people's reflections, a compilation of ingredients, the result of subtraction and a product of multiplication, pure mathematics. Neither Götz nor Meyer cared for math. They were simple people and loathed abstraction. What you see, exists, and what you don't see, doesn't exist, at least until you catch sight of it. Life was simple and there was no reason for it to get all tangled up like an unraveling sweater.

You could learn all sorts of things from the two of them. They knew, for instance, that the diameter of the movable exhaust pipe on their truck was fifty-eight to sixty millimeters wide, the diameter of the metal pipe welded to a hole of that size on the underside of the back part of the truck. And they knew that the fifteen or so kilometers they drove with their load every day was, in fact, an unnecessarily lengthy route, that the load could have been delivered earlier in the desired state. But they had no say in the matter, and as good members of the SS, they learned not to over-step their authority. How was it all explained to them? Was something drawn on a blackboard, with diagrams, letters, and arrows, or were they given a brief lecture couched in such vivid terms that no visual aids were needed? On the other hand, those five, or seven, Serbian prisoners knew nothing. How surprised they must have been when they first opened the back door of Götz and Meyer's truck and out billowed the dense, bluish cloud of poisonous gas! They stood there and stared at that sluggish cloud, which wafted lazily skyward, as if they were witnessing an act of divine revelation. They cocked back their heads and watched it float, and their jaws dropped farther and farther, as is often the case with the ignorant. Had Götz, or maybe Meyer, gone over to them then and said the word *hemoglobin*, they would have thought he was speaking Chinese. Only later, as if the cloud had held them back, the corpses began tumbling out. The prisoners snapped their mouths shut, but their eyes came out on stalks, and the veins on their necks bulged. One of them covered his nose, the second doubled over, the third prisoner's knees shook so much that from a distance he looked as if he'd been drinking. If the German guards hadn't shouted and used their rifle butts, who knows how long it would have taken for the Serbian prisoners to recover! Afterward they got used to it. A person gets used to everything, it doesn't matter whether he is a barbarian or a member of the master race. It took the Serbian prisoners less than an hour to do their job, I read that somewhere, quite good time, and fitted neatly into the overall requirement for frugality and efficiency in handling this, which was, after all, what the entire functioning of the Reich was based on. Despite this, Götz on that occasion, and undoubtedly Meyer as well, regretted the enforced confidentiality of the task, which prevented him from speaking briefly to those Serbs about the advantages of carbon monoxide. They were permitted to talk about this to Commander Andorfer, but Commander Andorfer had never been interested in such things. It is quite certain that, as a former hotelier, he knew nothing about chemistry. Carbon monoxide, Götz, or Meyer, might have said, is a colorless gas, without fragrance or taste, something lighter than air, and it is produced by the combustion of carbon, or a substance containing carbon, which occurs without sufficient oxygen. The rapid combustion of fuel in the truck's engine was an excellent example. Carbon monoxide condenses and turns into a liquid at temperatures of −192° Celsius, freezes at −199° Celsius, and melts at −205°. It is poisonous for all warm-blooded animals, which includes all human beings, with the exception of the Germans and the Japanese. As little as a thousandth of a percent of carbon monoxide in the air may provoke symptoms of poisoning – headaches, nausea, exhaustion – and a fifth of that same percent is lethal in less than half an hour. The speed of dying, obviously, increases in proportion to the increase in concentration of the gas, which proves beyond a shadow of a doubt Götz and Meyer's belief that an even shorter journey would have sufficed to ensure success. Now comes the part that Götz, or Meyer, would have enjoyed telling the most, if only he had been allowed to, and it has to do with the mechanism by which carbon monoxide acts in the blood of these animals: Russians, Jews, homosexuals, and mentally disabled

Germans, who weren't real Germans anyway, because a genuine member of the German race is physically, mentally, and sexually completely fit and always as he should be. Götz and Meyer were excellent specimens, especially Meyer, if not Götz as well, who had impeccably developed biceps, triceps, and glutei maximi. For a person to live, he needs oxygen, even those Serbian prisoners probably knew that, and he can absorb oxygen into his organism thanks to the presence of hemoglobin in his bloodstream. The oxygen forms bonds with the hemoglobin in the red blood cells, so that it is carried to all parts of the body. This hemoglobin, however, shows an unconcealed inclination to bond with carbon monoxide, which is as much as two to three hundred times as strong as its inclination to bond with oxygen, so, given the opportunity to choose, it will, like an unfaithful spouse, devote itself to the carbon monoxide. Once bonded, the hemoglobin and carbon monoxide create a stable compound of carboxyhemoglobin, which spreads quickly and reduces the amount of faithful hemoglobin that rushes into the embrace of pure oxygen. Without oxygen, of course, the pulse grows fainter, the respiratory system fails, tissues die like flies, coma sets in, and, in the end, so does death. The devastated organism is relieved that the torment is over, and death is salvation. Since carboxyhemoglobin has a characteristic cherry-red hue – Götz, or it could be Meyer, always clucks his tongue when referring to cherries – these asphyxiated victims do not turn blue as others do, rather their skin acquires a pinkish tinge and their lips turn bright red. This explains why the Serbian prisoners are thinking, "Lipstick," as the first heap of corpses tumbles toward them. They can guess why the women might be wearing lipstick, but they have not been able to explain to themselves why it is on the lips of the children and the elderly. In work such as theirs, however, you quickly learn not to ask questions, especially about Jews. Götz and Meyer wouldn't tell them anything about that anyway, not because they didn't know, but because there was no point in wasting words about Jews. It was enough that they had consumed so much fuel. I wouldn't be surprised if it turned out that the Jews themselves had paid for the fuel required for their transport from the Fairgrounds to Jajinci, since they'd paid for everything else so far, including food, medicine, and heating. The Belgrade archives hold the considerable correspondence between the Jewish Administration and the German Command Staff, with its competent services within the Municipality of Belgrade, regarding the procuring of foodstuffs, medicine, and the camp inventory. In the beginning I carefully copied out all the dates, and then I gave up, lost in the tons of food and cords of firewood, revolted by so much bureaucracy at a time when life was draining from the prisoners in the camp like water from wet rags. The setting up of the Jewish Administration was one of those sly tricks by which the Nazis organized their entire system of deceiving Jews, convincing them that the camps were merely reception centers on their way to some undesignated country, a huge ghetto that would belong to them alone. If something wasn't going well at the camp, then the only ones to blame would be the Jewish Administration. The Germans were here merely to help and advise, you could say nothing against them. Later, when Götz and Meyer went there, and their truck became a part of the dreary everyday routine of the camp prisoners, the members of the Administration and their families were saved until the last transport. No need to wonder why this was so: clearly the Administration had to oversee the schedule of departures to the end, the quality of the transportation, and the nutrition of those who still hadn't left. The same order of things would have held true in the real world, outside the camp, and as long as life in the camp was reminiscent, in no matter how reduced a form, of the life that was going on some-where else, chances are the prisoners would be calm and patient, waiting for their fate. This concern of the German government for the good of the pris-oners is touching, I think I've already said that, but at the Fairgrounds it did bear fruit. None of the incar-cerated Jews tried to run away, not even after the pattern had become clear and you needed much greater willpower to continue to deceive yourself. During the first three months, when hunger reigned in the camp, it was only some of the bolder little boys, judging by the statements of witnesses, who sneaked through the barbed-wire fence and went off to Zemun to beg for food. They knew that if they were caught as they slipped back in, they would be cruelly beaten, but their hunger was stronger. Hunger is always stronger, I dare say, although I have no experience of starvation, except for the fast at Yom Kippur, which I have been keeping stubbornly, though I can't say why, for the last twenty years. Götz and Meyer didn't know even that much about hunger, since they didn't know what Yom Kippur was. My guess is that they had never seen Jews either, espe-cially if they came from a small Austrian or German town, until they were given their special assignment. It is also my guess that among those who sneaked out through the barbed-wire fence there weren't any of my twelve young cousins, because I could never muster the strength to do something like that myself, and this leads me to believe, knowing my father's timidity and my mother's shyness, that this is a character trait handed down from one generation to the next in their families. Some people stride forward to embrace their fates; others, like my parents, wait for fate to come to them. It would not be good to conclude on the basis of this that the first is better than the other, because in the end fate is what counts, and not the circumstances leading up to it, just as one shouldn't think that I am dissatisfied with myself. I have found myself wondering sometimes whether things might have been different if there had been risk takers in our family tree, people from that first group. My mother's decision to go off to the village with me in her arms could be interpreted as taking a risk, but as I later learned in an entirely coincidental encounter in the rooms of the Jewish Historical Museum, she decided to do that only because she couldn't refuse a request from her best friend, also a Jewish woman and the mother of two little children, to go with her. This won't last long, her friend claimed, a few months and it will all blow over. They stayed, we stayed, in that village for more than three years, with my mother's constant complaints that it would have been so much better for her in Belgrade, even when the rumors reached them about the camp at the Fairgrounds. By then, however, it was no longer the Judenlager Semlin, but the Anhaltenlager Semlin – the Zemun Reception Camp – the Jews were all gone. Götz and Meyer had long since returned to Berlin with their incapacitated truck. What sort of group did they belong to, those who seek their fate or those who wait for it patiently, shifting from one foot to the other? For me every driver is someone seeking his own fate, if not provoking it, and this is why I have never learned to drive, but that cannot be taken as a yardstick in conditions of war. I must be fair to Götz and Meyer, I often thought, not only because of their cautious drive to Jajinci but just for the sake of being fair. They, too, had the right to be misled and hood-winked as much as the Jewish prisoners did, I can't possibly deny that. But all I had to do was picture one of them crouching to move the exhaust pipe of the truck over, and everything in me would be smashed to bits. Their load was still alive then, the trip had only just begun, and the brief stop did not arouse any doubts among the Jews. They were far more disturbed by the fact that they were traveling in the dark and that there was no room for them to get more comfortable. They felt the aluminum-covered walls and the wooden flooring, they touched each other and thanked the Lord that they weren't blind, it would be so terrible to live in eternal darkness, and then, with a shudder, the truck set off again, they could hear the engine rumbling good-naturedly, they could even smell the fuel, well that's all right, at least they were back on the road again, just so they'd never have to return to the cold and the hunger. If they could have, they probably would have shouted to Götz and Meyer to drive a little faster, to get as far from there as possible, to pay no attention to their nausea and mild headaches, surely from all the jouncing around and lack of fresh air, these were just little discomforts compared to what they were leaving behind. They had no idea how much farther and airier than anything they had imagined those distances would be. And Götz, and Meyer, drove along, whistling, exchanging jokes. Every job done according to a strictly defined formula becomes tedious in time. At first it is interesting, the second time confirms the first, by the fifth time it inspires annoyance, by the tenth it is routine, and by the fifteenth time Götz, or maybe it was Meyer, announces that he could drive to Jajinci with his eyes closed. Meyer, or was it Götz, who is always extracautious, feels that it is probably a better idea to drive with your eyes open, all it takes is for a cat to cross your path, not even a black one, and everything acquires a new dimension, a new meaning. Götz, or Meyer, shrugs this off. There is no such cat, he says, which could stop the victorious advance of the German Reich, not even in a land as wild as this Serbia is, where the cats scratch more than they did back in the Fatherland. Then they fall silent. Both of them are thinking of the cats they used to know: Götz, or maybe Meyer, thinks of a Siamese cat that his maiden aunt used to comb every day and feed with all sorts of treats, while Meyer, or maybe it was Götz, recalls a tiny striped cat that used to come into their garden, and he put its eye out with a stone from his slingshot. And then he sinks into fantasies about flying a fighter plane. It isn't nice, but there are times when he wishes that his fellow traveler would become ill, nothing too serious: a slightly worse cold with a bad cough, just enough so that he could be alone in the truck for one day, and then he'd put on his pilot's cap by the obligatory open window. It never happened, and if it did, there is no written trace of it. They were healthy lads, sturdy and resilient like all true members of the SS, not like those nobodies behind them to whom everything stuck like flies to flypaper. How much time had to pass for the required fifth of a percent to accumulate? And did the diameter of the exhaust pipe, no less than fifty-eight nor greater than sixty millimeters, have a part to play in this? What would have happened if it had been larger? Or smaller? Look at what I have been filling my head with since I turned fifty. I fill page after page with figures and information that I copy from books with fragile pages in archival cellars, although I have no idea what to do with most of it. For instance, on the basis of the report of the acting chief of the Section for Social Welfare and Social Institutions of the Municipality of Belgrade, written on April 17, 1942, precisely 1,341,950 meals were issued to feed Jews at the Fairgrounds camp. What do I divide that by? If I presume that there were 5,500 Jews at the camp on average every day, and that no food was delivered right from the very first day, it works out that every one of them received nearly two full meals per day, more precisely: 1.96 meals per day. But if one knows that the number of delivered meals is based on the total amount of delivered foodstuffs, most of which were not edible to begin with, that produces a rather different figure, around 1.3 meals per day. The food at the camp was served up with spoons of various sizes, only some of which corresponded to the standard of four deciliters, and this, as well as the fact that during April the number of prisoners dropped dizzyingly, sends this calculation into the sphere of higher mathematics, at least it does for me, a teacher of the Serbo-Croatian language and the literatures of the Yugoslav peoples. It is no wonder that I can't sleep night after night, and that in the morning, when I go down to the corner shop, I find myself counting loaves of bread in delivery crates, multiplying that number by the number of crates, and then multiplying that by the average weight of a loaf and, finally, dividing by 150 grams, which was what the prisoners at the Fairgrounds, according to the testimony of witnesses, received daily. One night, exhausted by all the figures, I dreamed of Götz, or maybe it was Meyer. We were sitting, he and I, in the cockpit of a fighter plane, crammed into the single pilot's seat, and he told me, in Serbian but with a strong German accent, the figures on the number of shells and machine-gun rounds, the fuel consumption, and the flight speed, and finally he turned to me and said that he had given away 327 chocolates. In my dream, just as when I'm awake, he had no face, the earflaps and ties on his pilot's cap framed a space of whiteness. Only his lips were bright red, as if he had applied a thick layer of lipstick. I leaned over and looked out of the window, and below, quite clearly,

I could see the blueprints for the Belgrade Fair, precisely as it was imagined by the architects Milivoje Tričković, Rajko Tatić and Djordje Lukić. And now, said Götz, or maybe it was Meyer, we will look at all of this up close, the plane began to plummet with a piercing whine, straight for the blueprint of the Central Tower, and, with a shriek, I woke. I lay in the dark, afraid to breathe. But if before I could have been in a plane, now I might be in the back of the Saurer, and the longer I held my breath, the longer I'd be able to preserve my soul. How long can a person hold his breath? Half a minute, one minute, two? I counted to thirty-eight to myself, my lungs bursting. I gasped and gulped greedily at the air. In the flat above me I could hear soft footsteps and knew that it was my soul, cloaked in a garment of the thinnest light, moving lightly along a path I still had to discover. Götz and Meyer wouldn't care for this frequent mention of souls, as I have said before. According to them, a person is a sack, and when everything is shaken out of the sack, it is over. All that is left is the rag, and rags are no good for anything. Sometimes, when they'd clean out the truck in the yard of the police station, Götz and Meyer would find odds and ends: a child's shoe, a comb, a blurred photograph, a crust of bread, a handkerchief, a nail file, a brooch.

Götz, or Meyer, would drop these things into a paper bag; Meyer, or Götz, preferred not to touch them. Nothing sadder than things without owners, even he knew that, just as he knew that the time of the Reich was a time of joy and little things like these dared not degrade it. How old were Götz and Meyer? One more question I can't answer. When one of my students is unable to answer a question, for example on the structure of a wreath of sonnets, I do not hesitate to enter, first in my notebook and then in the register, a bad grade. If I were to apply the same criteria to myself, I would have been held back long ago. So it goes with history, the woman told me from whom I'd heard the story about my mother. She compared history to a big crossword puzzle. For every little square you fill, there are three more empty, she said, and even if you manage to fill them, new ones open up immediately, even emptier. Knowledge can never catch up with the power of ignorance. It seemed to me that I had read that somewhere before, but I no longer had the strength to open new little empty squares in myself. That was what I said to the woman who sat across from me and in whose spectacles I could clearly see my own baffled countenance reflected. She shook her head sadly. It is terrible, she said, to live in history, and even more terrible to live outside it. If she had given me the precise solution to my crossword puzzle, she couldn't have surprised me more. I saw how the face reflected in her glasses – or, in fact, two identical faces side by side – shuddered and licked their lips, powerless to come up with any sort of response. In the end I mumbled that it reminded me of the folktale about the dark lands. History is a dark land, the woman smiled, you're damned if you venture in and damned if you don't. Whatever you do you'll regret it forever. I said nothing. Even Götz, or Meyer, couldn't extricate me from that one. For a while longer I poked around in the volumes of documents, as if I were sorting through grains of rice to pick out the pebbles, and then I slipped outside, afraid that if I stayed, I'd lose myself completely in the lenses of her glasses. I walked down 7th of July Street clutching my satchel with papers and books under my arm, and turned into Gospodar Jovanova Street. According to a variety of sources, as many as four of my relatives lived here with their families. One of them was the man Haim, later gloriously renamed Benko, the only one for whom I knew the date of death. Or, more precisely: I could place the date of his death within the four or five days when they were exterminating the doctors and patients of the Jewish hospital in Visokog Stevana Street, which seems pretty precise compared with the span of fifty days or so during which the transports went on from the Fairgrounds camp. When the rest of Belgrade's Jews were transported to the camp on December 8, 1941, the staff and patients at the Jewish hospital were spared. Apparently – a poor word to use when speaking of history, I realize that, but it cropped up from the empty little squares of the crossword puzzle – so, apparently, there was a plan to move the entire hospital to the Nikola Spasić Foundation pavilion, which never happened, although part of the hospital's equipment was moved to that pavilion, to the camp infirmary, so that the medical staff, at least temporarily and ostensibly, was spared the horrors of residing at the camp. The Jewish hospital was opened in the summer of 1941, and during the winter months it quickly filled with patients from the camp, so that by March 1942, when Götz and Meyer's truck docked at its door like some big boat, there were about five hundred patients at the hospital. The day before, all the Jewish doctors and other staff had been arrested, with their families, and all of them were also being held at the hospital, putting the total number at over seven hundred souls. By March 22 or possibly 23, the hospital was empty, and the souls were wafting through the spacious skies over Jajinci. There is an assumption – yet another word unsuited to history – that this was a sort of rehearsal for the much larger and more serious job at the Fairgrounds, and it is certain that Götz and Meyer did their job well, and that Schäfer, Andorfer, and Enge and many other leaders could breathe a sigh of relief, and even pat each other on the back. One can therefore conclude that Götz and Meyer had arrived in Belgrade two or three days earlier, so they did not have a chance to see the town, although they would certainly do so later, mostly from the truck but also on short strolls, which Götz was better at, though it may have been Meyer. Meyer, or possibly Götz, preferred to sleep in his spare time, and he never complained that his dreams disturbed him. You couldn't say the same for Götz, or was it Meyer, who often awoke at night, sometimes making a lot of noise, and then he'd go out for a walk to get a bit of fresh air. I doubt that his conscience played any part in this, I'm inclined to attribute it all to poor digestion. Haim himself, as a doctor, would have said as much to Götz, or Meyer, had he only had the opportunity to ask him amid the pandemonium when they loaded everyone onto the truck in front of the Jewish hospital. There was none of this tumult a few days later when the same truck began stopping in at the Fairgrounds. Here things were quiet, and there was even enthusiasm at the thought of leaving, which certainly pleased Götz and Meyer, and they made no effort to hide it. Everyone likes being appreciated in the workplace, why not Götz and Meyer? Meyer even confessed to me that he felt his heart beat faster and that later, when he recalled those days, he would shiver. Look at this: I am beginning to imagine myself talking with people whose faces I don't even know. I knew precious little, indeed, about the faces of most of my kin, but in their case I can at least look at my own face in the mirror and seek their features there, whereas with Götz and Meyer I had no such help. Anyone could have been Götz. Anyone could have been Meyer, and yet Götz and Meyer were only Götz and Meyer, and no one else could be who they were. It is hardly surprising, therefore, that I constantly had this feeling that I was slipping, even when I was walking on solid ground. The void that was Götz and Meyer so contrasted with the fullness of my relatives, if not of their real beings at least of their deaths, that my every attempt to reach fullness required that first I had to pass through void. For me to truly understand real people like my relatives, I had first to understand unreal people like Götz and Meyer. Not to under-stand them: to conjure them. Sometimes I simply had to become Götz, or Meyer, so I could figure out what Götz, or Meyer (really I), thought about what Meyer, or Götz (really I), meant to ask. This Götz who was not really Götz spoke to this Meyer who was not really Meyer. My hands tremble a little when I think of it all. Nothing easier than to stray into the wasteland of someone else's consciousness. It is more difficult to be master of one's own fate; simpler to be master of someone else's. In the morning, while I dressed, I'd be Götz and Meyer. I did not allow myself to be distracted by details, for instance: wondering whether German soldiers wore short-sleeved undershirts, or dog tags with their personal details round their necks. I always wore tank tops, cut high under the armpits, important because I sweat so much, and nothing was going to make me stop wearing them. This was about something else. I would look at myself, let's say, in the mirror and say: Now Meyer is combing his hair, and then Götz would ask Meyer what he'd be having for breakfast. Once I got up in a foul mood, as Götz, and when asked that same question, told Meyer angrily: bananas. Lord, how Meyer laughed. His razor bounced around in his hand! Later, when he rinsed off the foam, he noticed a little nick on his left cheek, but that only reminded him of Götz's reply, and then he burst into guffaws again. Götz didn't say anything, because by then he was already in the kitchen, where he watched as I made coffee. Quite the bright one, that Götz, never to put the cart before the horse. As they drove toward Belgrade, he never carped to Meyer, possibly Götz, about speeding. It is important to tend to state property entrusted to your care, but even more important to tend to good relations with your work colleagues, since your success in completing any assignment depends far more on that than on anything else. Speaking of carts and horses, I should say that Götz and Meyer fussed over their Saurer as if it were some rare thoroughbred horse: they groomed it, cleaned and washed it, changed its tires as if they were horseshoes, filled it with the finest fuel, and if there had been a way for them to give it sugar cubes, I am sure they would have done. You can hardly blame them for being so dejected when the Saurer's rear axle broke. Götz and Meyer were only human, after all. I have a feeling that the woman at the Jewish Historical Museum didn't like that. She was silent for so long, looking right into my eyes, that in the end I wondered if she hadn't heard me so I repeated what I had said. Indeed they were, said the woman, there can be no doubt about that. But what sort of human? It is incredible, the degree to which other people are so much better at grasping the essence of something that eludes us. Really, what sort of human beings were Götz and Meyer? What kind of man would, like the two of them, consent to do a job that meant putting five or six thousand souls to death? I find it hard to give a student a bad grade at the end of the semester, let alone at the end of the year, but that is nothing compared to the way Götz and Meyer must have felt. Or what if they felt nothing at all? I could stare all I wanted to in the mirror, to fill the voids of their faces with mine, but I still couldn't come up with an answer. I went over to the family tree hanging on the wall, framed like some sort of abstract drawing. As always I felt only pain, a dull pain, I started losing breath, gasping like a carp out of water, and I could do nothing but rush outdoors, although all those walks ended up with my going to stand in front of one of the houses where my relatives used to live, or to the Fairgrounds, where I tried to picture the ice. That winter, the winter between 1941 and 1942, was so cold, it is no wonder some of the prisoners said openly that everyone, even God, had forsaken them. No matter how many clothes you wore, no matter how thick your coat or cloak, the cold would creep into your limbs and find its way to your heart. And when the heart is cold, there is no fire hot enough to warm you. The fire that burned in the heaters in the Fairgrounds pavilions could hardly have warmed limbs, let alone hearts. In vain the camp administration sent letters to the Municipality of Belgrade requesting larger amounts of firewood and, on one occasion, ten wedges for splitting stumps. A stump is a stump, and experienced woodsmen would give up on those knots that skewed saw teeth and blunted axes. The children wept, the elderly died, the women who went off to forced labor lost chunks of flesh and patches of skin from their arms. It was enough to bump into something, a witness said, and frostbite would form there immediately. I am someone who gets cold easily, and at the very thought of how cold it was my teeth start chattering; even tea couldn't warm me then. Even today, for instance, my ear hurts where it froze, once, when I was a boy on the Tara Mountain. It's my left ear, I often stroke the left lobe while I teach new material. Twelve years ago on television they showed a detective comedy involving Freemasons, and, at least in that series, they would recognize one another by touching their left earlobe. Ever since then, the students have called me Freemason. Did Götz and Meyer have nicknames? Would it change anything if I were to learn that their wives, if they were married, had pet names for them, something like Teddy Bear or Big Boy? By the way, in a list of Belgrade Freemasons I found the names of three of my relatives, two from my father's side and one from my mother's. There are secret threads that always surface, you just have to be patient. I count the frostbitten ear as one such thread, but also the fact that as a boy, I liked to stand behind cars and breathe in what I now know to be poisonous fumes. A small amount of carbon monoxide produces a mild sense of dizziness, and I probably found in that sensation a little joy or comfort in a world that, even then, seemed far too hostile, strict, and rigid. I am referring to the things, of course, that make the world what it is, not politics, I want to be sure that is perfectly clear. I knew nothing at that point about politics, or about the gas truck; after all, when I first happened upon the term "soul-swallower" in reference to the truck, my initial association was with some mythical creature, a being that delighted in plucking the feathers of life from weeping souls the way women plucked feathers from butchered chickens. In one sense, you might say, I was right, only because in a "soul-swallower" truck the soul plucks its own feathers in a bid to shed its ballast as soon as possible and soar skyward, as high as possible, where the air is still pure. In an encyclopedia

I found a map marking all the places where gas trucks were used by the SS. Most of the places were within the Soviet Union, a dozen in the Reich, and in only one case did the little dots upset the balance and dip southward to Belgrade and the Fairgrounds. Seven hundred thousand people, it said in that same encyclopedia, were killed in those vehicles, and that means that since some thirty gas trucks were produced, here I go calculating again, on average around twenty thousand people were asphyxiated in each. The calculation is incomplete because it does not consider the differences in capacity between the two models, the Saurer and the Diamond, but I wasn't able to work that out. If I had a better grasp of mathematics, I wouldn't be teaching literature, in which, unlike any true science, every interpretation has equal value, while as you increase precision you decrease overall quality, or, rather, you undermine the work itself. If a literary work is not in constant motion, I told my students, then it is not a work but a blind alley of the human spirit. The students nodded, their pencils hurried along the lines on their notebook pages, their lips silently repeated the thought I had just voiced. The first gas trucks were used in November 1941, in Ukraine, and then they dispersed in all directions: to Leningrad, Sebastopol, Berlin, Majdanek, Lvov,

Piatigorsk, Danzig, and Vienna. In comparison with these vast expanses, Götz and Meyer's journey to Belgrade seems like a little side trip, perhaps needless or hasty, especially if you keep in mind the smallness of the job and the digression from the already established routes of movement. But some things are logical precisely because they cannot be explained by any other logic, right? Exactly, Götz and Meyer are logical precisely because they defy all other logic, as I don't doubt that woman from the Jewish Historical Museum would say, with her glasses on or off, same difference. I resemble to myself that old rabbi of Prague who built a manlike creature of clay and breathed life into it, with the difference that I am trying to construct Götz and Meyer out of airy memories, unreliable recollection, and crumbling archival documents. We know how the rabbi's experiment turned out: the clay being rebelled against its creator, the rabbi just barely managed, standing on his toes, to erase one of the letters inscribed on the creature's forehead, changing the word *life* to the word *death*. Is that what I want to do: to bring Götz and Meyer back to the shadows in the former Fairgrounds camp, to give them life so that, quickly, quickly, I make them die? The moral, however, of the Prague story is clear: no one should play God, not a rabbi, not a writer, not a narrator, and words, no matter how powerful, can never replace the silence of God's creation. Even if I were to oppose them, what would I do if Götz and Meyer, intoxicated with their new life, went mad and took up where they'd left off with their old work? There aren't many Jews left in Belgrade, but the number doesn't matter, what matters is the conviction, there would be work here, of course. Would I then be able to reach their foreheads, Götz and Meyer's foreheads, and what would I erase: wrinkles, drops of sweat, the hair in their eyes? I am a squeamish man, I would have to use a handkerchief. Götz and Meyer would be so scornful! I would become an object of ridicule, stories about me would make the rounds in the barracks and the execution grounds, and Götz, though possibly Meyer, would imitate my gesture at the officers' mess over and over again, patting a folded napkin against his forehead like a powder puff. I hope no one will think I'm mad, though even I find it difficult to convince myself I'm not. Sometimes right in the middle of a class, I stop talking, stare at the tip of my pen or a pattern on the grimy windowpane, and don't even finger my left earlobe. When I catch myself, I see thirty-two pairs of eyes fixed on me, unblinking. How can I explain to them that I am a living example of parallel literary worlds, that I am a protagonist from books that have not yet been written? How do I make it clear that I am made up of a plenitude of empty little squares and not a word will ever be written in any of them? That my life is becoming more and more hollow with each passing day, and that one day, perhaps right there in front of their eyes, I will float up like a balloon and remain wedged beneath the ceiling? My students are nice, they would run at once to shut the windows. But I keep opening them. I go over to the family tree, framed, hanging on the wall, and stare at it as if I am seeing it for the first time, I clamber from branch to branch, hop all the way across the treetop, feel as if all those young and old dead people are filling me, choking me, how they cluster like wasps on the hemoglobin in my blood, and then I rush to the window, fling it open, hoping I'll set the opposite process in motion and free my hemoglobin from danger, that oxygen will flood my mind once more. There I stand by the open window and fill my lungs with air. I live in one of those modern neighborhoods, and when I look outside, I see only the high-rises across the way and a patch of sky. The sky over the Fairgrounds is far larger, and by the same token more hopeless, which, actually, was a comfort to the prisoners at the camp, because when the sky is close, then life is very far away. I don't know where I read that, maybe I've made it all up, there is no mention of sky in any of the witness statements. But who could think of something so ephemeral, surrounded by barbed wire and caught between the freezing cold and starvation? Now Götz, on the other hand, or Meyer, loved looking up at the sky, especially at clouds, and often, even while they were driving, he would try to get Meyer, if it wasn't Götz after all, to spot all sorts of shapes in them: an elephant, for instance, or a zeppelin. Meyer, or maybe it was Götz, got so tired of his pestering once that he told Götz, or was it Meyer he told, that he'd better stop it. He didn't so much say this as bark it at him like a high-ranking Gestapo officer. The veins on his neck bulged, his face went red, globules of spit sprayed between his clenched teeth and splattered the cab. Even men with nerves of steel, powerful and reliable in every way, have weak moments. Götz, or Meyer, stopped talking, pouted like a child, didn't even want to eat his dinner. He was sorry he hadn't brought along his book of poetry, nothing was as soothing as a nice verse. At breakfast the next day, however, all was well again, they told each other the dreams they'd dreamed the night before, as they always did, and precisely at the scheduled time the Saurer stopped at the gate to the camp. They've come, they've come, the whispers spread among the children, not the ones, of course, who were already standing in the line, selected for the transport, with their mothers, with the occasional father as well, there still were a few Jewish fathers alive, not, therefore, among those children, but among the others, the ones whose turn was going to come in a few days, and now they were scampering about, along the barbed wire and among the pavilions, it was among them that the whispers circulated, the hope that in the magic circle of chocolates that morning some of them would be the select few. You take the chocolate on your tongue, press it up into the roof of your mouth, let the taste spread all through you. At that same time, the little company of gravediggers was busily digging the grave in Jajinci, although it looked more like a ditch, not too deep and not too shallow, spacious enough for about a hundred people. They dug in silence. The soil was good, moist, all manner of things would flourish in it. According to one witness statement, eighty-one or eighty-two ditches were dug, and that was only for those Jews who arrived in the Saurer, day after day, sometimes twice in a day. For those who were shot by firing squads, there were special graves, special ditches, I don't know why, that witness didn't know either, he couldn't recall the dimensions, but killing, too, is an art, and it has its own rules, and it is one thing, I guess, when you lower an asphyxiated person into the ground, and something else again when the person, weighed down by the bullet in his heart, drops into the void. The gravediggers, of course, wasted no time on thoughts like that. It was their task to dig, and they dug. Time was precious, at any moment the Saurer might appear from round the bend, the gravediggers would leave, and from another truck, a military truck, four German guards would hop out with five, or seven, Serbian prisoners, and, actually, all of them were thinking the same thing: when will night come, when will night finally come? Several days later, leaning on the truck while Commander Andorfer smoked and the Serbian prisoners moved the corpses, Götz, or Meyer, as if it mattered, couldn't stop himself and asked why they had to drive these revolting Jews, wouldn't it be better to do all this closer to the camp, the truck could do what it did standing still, that would be, if he dared be so bold as to observe, far more economical. Untersturmführer Andorfer stopped midstride and thought about it. Then he had a puff on his cigarette and asked what they would do then with the processed individuals, they couldn't stay forever in that truck, could they? Götz, or Meyer, hadn't considered that and said the first thing that came to mind: they could toss them in the river. Andorfer winced with disgust. We are not barbarians, he said, if we have been called upon to give people a better life, then we should also give them a finer death. Götz, or Meyer, shrugged, he had nothing to say against an argument like that, and he was even sorry he'd made the suggestion in the first place. It was his job to drive, to reconnect the exhaust pipe to the opening on the underside of the truck, and later to clean the truck out and polish it for a new load. Why did he need to get involved in something that was none of his business? Precisely, said Andorfer as if he knew how to read minds. Later that afternoon, while he was playing cards with members of the Jewish Administration, his hand trembled and drops of coffee splashed the black king of spades and the red two of diamonds. Such are the times, you never know who will stab you in the back, and where, and when. Shivers traveled up and down his spine, there was an itch under his shoulder blades. I get itchy in that same place, I know the feeling. When it happens to me in my flat, it's not so bad: I lean on the door frame and scratch myself like a wild boar, but when I'm in the classroom, standing in front of my students, the itching throws me into indescribable torment. That is when I grab my left earlobe on purpose, drawing their attention to that Masonic gesture, and meanwhile secretly twisting my right arm behind my back and pushing my thumb hard into the itchy spot, as if I really did plan to drill straight through. There isn't a student in the classroom that moment hoping more than I that the bell will ring for the end of class. I went to see a dermatologist who explained politely that most things that appear on the human body in the form of eczema, boils, red patches, and, of course, itchy spots, no matter where they break out, are treated somewhere altogether different. I looked at him, curious, and he placed his index finger to his temple. Was there a history in my family of any sort of disease, the dermatologist wanted to know. His index finger was still pointing to his temple. Most of them died of poisoning, I said. There are some truths people simply will not believe, there is no point in trying to convince them. The dermatologist became serious and, though it was difficult for him, I could see, to pull his index finger away from his temple, he prescribed some sort of ointment for me, recommended bathing frequently, using mild soaps, eating as many fresh vegetables as I could manage, and going for walks in the countryside. I went off to the Fairgrounds. When I was there, my entire body itched, but still that was easier to take.

Belgrade was resting over there across the river. It was not, of course, the same city the prisoners had stared at hungrily, but it was silent in just the same way. No, that's not right, I am not telling the truth: there were presentiments, guesses, rumors circulated, people noticed the absences, corpses were seen wrapped in sheets, but no one did anything, no one even tried to do anything. What could they have done? Would I have done something had I been in their place? Or would I have buried my head in the sand, happy that I even had a head and that sand still existed? I probably would have done just that, I certainly would have been an ostrich, everyone's world was shifting then, everyone was learning to live from the beginning again. You can't judge a man until you've walked a mile in his shoes, isn't that true? No, said the woman I met at the Jewish Historical Museum, but I preferred not to argue with her. I didn't want to argue with anyone. History was a millstone, a millstone doesn't think why it is grinding grain. I pictured Götz and Meyer all white, covered in flour, and couldn't help but laugh. What a laugh it would have been for the children at the camp to see their white figures! Even more droll than Götz's, or Meyer's, little poodle with a bow on its head. The children would have been even more delighted had more than the amount of milk allotted for daily consumption, more than the regular thirty liters, been delivered. If you count how many children and infants there were at the camp, it works out that every child got a spoonful. After making that calculation, I couldn't eat dairy products for several weeks. The trembling density of yogurt made me nauseous, while the amount of milk you needed to moisten oat flakes seemed like needless waste. Without the milk and dairy products I had consumed, so to say, my whole life, I felt like a drug addict without my favorite drug. My hands shook, the chalk crumbled in my fingers, my eyes filled with tears, my legs refused to obey me, words lodged in my throat. Sometimes I would stand motionless for hours, rigid and trembling, and then for days I couldn't stop moving, I was moving constantly, as if all the world's furies were after me. I only recovered when I read in a book that the quality of the food in the camp improved dramatically in early March. There was no mention of milk, per se, but the prisoners did receive three barrels of marmalade. I am assuming that this was marmalade made from mixed fruit, which would suit all tastes, and all possible different preferences, in equal measure. I rushed off to the market and purchased a pint of sour cream, which I later ate spoonful by spoonful until I got sick. The improvement in the quality of food, it said in the book, and there are statements from witnesses to back this up, was accompanied by a change in the behavior of the German soldiers and camp command. The earlier nasty treatment disappeared, or at least lessened, the humiliation and punishments stopped, some officers even began smiling. At that point, the stories of transfer to some other camp, in Romania or Poland, or even to a warm island somewhere, became almost real, tangible, and the nights got shorter somehow, passed quicker in guessing and dissuading, melting into days that no longer brought so much anxiety and uncertainty. Commander Andorfer showed the members of the Jewish Administration the rules of the camp, there was no longer any reason to hide them, he hadn't hidden them earlier, he claimed, he simply hadn't known they were there, so that he, too, you could see just by looking at him, had been pleasantly surprised. As a sign of gratitude, I guess, they let him win at cards for several days running. Meanwhile, Götz and Meyer were also preparing to travel. If they were married, they whispered tender words to their wives, if they had children, they promised they would be home soon, bringing presents. Nothing big, of course, children needn't be exposed from a young age to luxury that might only damage them later in life. Geometrically speaking, Götz and Meyer were moving along a horizontal route that would allow the Jews at the Fairgrounds camp to begin their vertical journey. It would seem, of course, that they, the Jews, would be traveling horizontally as well, but the path they'd be taking would head upward, skyward. In historical terms, the departure of the Saurer with Götz and Meyer from Berlin marked the end of a debate of many months on the fate of the Jews in Belgrade and Serbia. Certain Nazi officials wanted to transfer them eastward, to one of the newly formed ghettoes or camps; others, obviously more traditionally minded, felt that they should continue with the firing squads; at the very top, however, the spirit of modernity reigned supreme, and there was a readiness to continue providing support for the development of a more humane and painless form of killing. Finally, when it was all put down on paper and compared – the price of ammunition, and the costs of transport, and the number of soldiers necessary for it to function without a hitch, and the amount of food and other supplies, and the unquestionable influences on the psyches of those involved – it was clear that the most efficient method, as those people insisted who believed in the advancement of scientific thought, was to send a gas truck to Belgrade. Two drivers, four guards, and five, or seven, prisoners: a dozen people was all they needed to strike one problem off the agenda. Even if one were to add to that the work of the grave- and ditch diggers, it still cost less than organizing the transport and overly long and sometimes chaotic shootings. I had to admit that one rarely comes across such crystal-clear and iron-firm logic. Had I been able to apply similar logic to my life, it probably wouldn't have looked like a messy train schedule gone awry, which was the nearest image of its, or rather my, condition. This was best seen in my attempt to bring order to myself by introducing order to my family tree, and it all ended in nothing but even greater trouble. I wrote letters to my relatives in Australia, Israel, America, and Argentina. I introduced myself, apologized for not having written for such a long time, I believe I even remarked that we were the last kernels on a gnawed ear of corn, and then I asked them whether they could tell me anything that might help me to better understand events that, I confess, defy comprehension, but which must have had some sort of meaning, because if they didn't, then our lives, or at least mine, would be meaningless. No one responded. At eighty and some, their average age, you are grateful that day and night and tangible things still exist, you no longer ask yourself why you are alive. But nonetheless several times a day I would peer into my letter box, hoping for the postman's mercy the way a believer prays for a voice from above. I would grasp at the tiniest straw, I admit, just as the prisoners grasped at the straw of the stories they had heard from Commander Andorfer. We'll be sorry, I told my students, if we ever stop telling stories because if we do, there will be nothing to help us sustain the pressure of reality, to ease the burden of life on our shoulders. Almost at the same moment, as if on command, all of them stopped writing and looked up at me. But, they asked, isn't life a story? No, I answered, and touched my earlobe, life is the absence of story. Nonsense, said Meyer, or possibly Götz. We were sitting under a willow tree, smoking. I wasn't sure what he was referring to, but I knew that there were plenty of things I would rather be talking about with him than the purpose of narration. I was thinking of life, Meyer announced, or was it Götz?, and shrugged in his attempt to get rid of a cloud of midges and mosquitoes. It is more precious, he added, than you think, much more precious, believe me, I know what I'm talking about. This had gone too far! A man with no face who has channeled death in the direction of thousands of men, women, and children's bodies with his own hands is explaining the value of life to me, in admonishing tones, no less! Perhaps I should have taken that dermatologist's index finger a little more seriously? I wrote new letters to my relatives scattered round the continents. Did they have any idea, I asked in these letters, of any illness, not counting poisoning, that belonged to us like some family treasure? No one answered, the postman began avoiding me. I would go out to wait for his arrival at the entrance, and he would detour all the way round the block of flats and sneak in through the back door. I would be standing on the street corner and he would trot by on the pavement opposite. His mailbag bounced and banged against his buttocks. In the end he started wearing ordinary clothes and carrying the post in an ordinary carrier bag. He even took off his postman's cap and stuffed it in his pocket. Götz, or Meyer, the one who dreamed he might become a pilot, had no doubts. It may be that the uniform does not make the man, which I do not believe myself, he said sternly, but working on the assumption that this is so, you cannot say the same for headgear. At that he gazed fondly at the pilot's cap hanging in the cab, right behind him. When he leaned his head back, the leather ties tickled his neck softly. But what about those people who don't wear caps? I, for instance, wore a cap with a visor as a kid. Now I go bareheaded, summer and winter. My father went bareheaded, so did my mother, except when she did the housekeeping: then she'd put on a kerchief. I leafed through the pictures in our family album. My father had a hat in only one of them, but he was holding it. I sat down and wrote a new round of letters to my relatives, asking them to describe any caps they had, if they had any. No one responded. When I pounced out of the cellar and interrupted the postman, he was terrified, tried to hit me with the carrier bag crammed with letters and newspapers, and threatened to report me to the police. Commander Andorfer was no nicer. He forbade all writing of letters, he shouted to the lined-up prisoners, and if anyone was caught writing a letter or sending it, they would be punished most severely. From the so-called block commanders, who maintained order in the pavilions, and the camp police, most of them youngish women responsible for discipline, they expected full cooperation. Indeed, just as the Jews fed themselves, so they also guarded themselves. If something went wrong, they had no one else to blame, least of all the Germans. The Germans were here, as Commander Andorfer explained, to help them and, most important, to free them of the responsibility for punishing those who broke the rules, for instance, anyone who wrote letters or carried letters out of the camp. So it was, for the purpose of making an example, that the courier who used to go to the Jewish hospital on Dorćol every day, and through whom the prisoners sent letters to their ailing relatives and friends, was shot. He was shot on the grounds of the camp, not for the sake of us Germans, as Scharführer Fritz Stracke, director of the Jewish Office within the Belgrade Gestapo, said on the occasion, but for your sake, and therefore, he raised his index finger and paused dramatically, be prudent! However, every student is not a good student, a subject I would have something to say about, not even when attending real-life classes. Letters kept going to Belgrade, so two more women were shot in January 1942. In February another five or six women were shot, and then a girl. Obstinacy, Andorfer said, is bad for the health. Götz and Meyer were already on the outskirts of Belgrade at that point, and when they arrived, the letter-writing stopped. There was no longer any need to inform the world outside the camp, or rather, every person was gradually becoming a letter that, with no address, sped swiftly and reliably to its destination. Persistence always produces results, thought Andorfer while the cool breeze ruffled his hair at Jajinci. In my case, however, obstinacy failed, and not only in the realm of letter-writing. By the way, I no longer sent letters to my relatives, I sent them postcards. I never managed to find a nice view of the Fairgrounds, so I sent them a panoramic shot taken from Kalemegdan, which showed Zemun and New Belgrade. None of them ever responded. People began looking at me suspiciously at the archives and museums, their kindness gave way to distrust, their friendliness to intolerance. The lonely family tree dropped off the wall one night and crashed to the floor. I leaped out of bed, tripped, fell, and gashed my forehead on the arm of a chair. The cut wasn't large, I managed to stop the bleeding, but the next morning, at the infirmary, they put a piece of gauze on my forehead and attached it with a bandage. Marked, I walked around town wondering whether that was how the Jews felt when they had to wear the six-pointed star on their sleeve or on their lapel. The more I tried to be unnoticeable, the more the patch on my forehead gleamed and enunciated mutely, yet distinctly, This is he, this is he. Who am I? Good question, said that woman at the Jewish Historical Museum. When you find an answer to that one, she added, you will answer all the rest. I didn't know what questions she was referring to. Götz and Meyer didn't either. I'd like to see them with that white badge and ask them how they feel. It was about then, when summer was well along the way, that I began to give up. I'd get up listless, broken, every bone in my body ached, and the simplest effort, tying my shoelaces, for instance, turned into an unbearable trial. I stood before a glass wall, best to put it that way, and no matter what shoes I was wearing, no matter what I used to steady myself, I could not find a way to climb up and out. I slid, slid, and it got worse just when I thought I had finally figured out how to get a hold on the edge. Some things never can be grasped, and perhaps it is better that they stay that way, mean-inglessness being their only meaning. A group of men, for instance, take seats around a table and decide to wipe out an entire people. There are some doubts here, although they are purely technical in nature, questions need to be answered beginning with the words *when*, *how*, and *where*, but no one questions the initial assumption anymore. With its meaning-lessness it forges new meaning, crystal clear, and there-after that is held up as the measure of all other meaning. You are on the right track, say Götz and Meyer, and wink at me in unison. I'd never seen Götz and Meyer, I could only imagine them. I imagined them hacking at chunks of mountain crystal with powerful blows and building the wall before which I stand, fifty years later, a limp little lamb. I'm sure that this notion of immutable transparency occurred to those prisoners, back then, but they saw themselves inside some sort of glass ball, exposed to the world's uncaring eyes, teetering on the brink of a downward slope. Their ball rolled away, my wall stood there, still. Then I remembered that I'd read somewhere that there are no outer walls, only inner ones, and that we must climb out from inside if we wish to overcome what rises before us outside. Okay, okay, I said to Götz and Meyer, who were nodding eagerly, but how can someone proceed if he has never even discovered the way that leads to the outer doors? Götz and Meyer shook their heads helplessly. Perhaps I am expecting too much of them, they are, after all, only ordinary people, practical, skilled at something that requires no questions or answers. And what is so bad about that, asks Götz, or maybe Meyer, in a tone bordering on the surly, and is there anyone who knows, who genuinely knows, that he wouldn't act precisely the same way in our place? I don't know what to answer him and whether there is such an answer. I don't know why I am talking with him in front of the prisoners scowling at us through the barbed-wire fence. They are convinced that I am getting in the way of their departure that started out so nicely, that I am dissuading the people who, with their arrival from far away, have brought a glimmer of light into the prisoners' lives. And indeed, at first, when Götz and Meyer's Saurer arrived, the prisoners raced to see who would be the first to travel. Commander Andorfer, I imagine, must have rubbed his hands with glee. Later, when some of the members of the Jewish Administration had begun to show some doubt, Andorfer fumed and, his language harsh, leaning on his arms as he spoke, said that doubt was one of the greatest human frailties, he wanted no weaklings in his camp, whatever would become of the Reich if the Führer allowed himself to be enticed, even for a moment, by doubt, and would he, Andorfer, be sitting with them had he doubted his own words, and why doesn't someone deal out those cards? But doubt is like sourdough: once you make it, it keeps rising. Since Götz and Meyer's truck always stood outside the camp, and only the select had access to it, the prisoners, according to witness statements, tried to make use of another truck, the one for transporting each group's personal belongings. They agreed that when the trucks reached their destination, the people who had been taken away were to leave a message in a predetermined spot inside the truck, letting the others know where they had been unloaded. It couldn't be so hard to do, surely they would be unloading their own things from the truck, certainly the Germans wouldn't be doing something like that for them, but no search of the truck, when it returned to the camp the next day, ever produced any sort of result. The dead, of course, don't write. Souls communicate in a different tongue. But there were always those for whom this meant nothing, for whom proof was not proof, after all penciled messages are so easily misplaced and dust can parch the lips. Nothing had changed, nothing could change. The women and children, the occasional elderly person, sometimes even a man or two, and one of the medical staff continued climbing up, day after day, into the Saurer, though with flagging enthusiasm. Commander Andorfer ordered that if there weren't enough volunteers, they would start drawing up transport lists, but everything continued as planned, without much resistance, without a fuss, because as long as there was hope, there was a chance it might be borne out, wasn't there? And besides, nothing warms hope like a full stomach, and in April and May 1942, judging by the documents that have been preserved, there were no complaints about the amount and quality of the delivered food. Since the number of prisoners was dropping, they were all finally being served with spoons of the same size, the stew was thicker, the bits of potato more numerous, the corn mush a little less watery. Some children even got candy two or three times from Götz, or Meyer, which would have been unthinkable before. I asked Götz, or possibly Meyer, why the sweets, didn't that seem just a tad hypocritical? No, said Götz, or possibly Meyer, because when a person works at a monotonous job, he needs some respite, otherwise there is the danger that he might lose his élan and, worst of all, that he might ultimately turn into an automaton, which, though precise, would function with less of a will. Indeed, I concede. We talked in my room. A recording of Mozart's music was playing on the turntable. We sat and smoked and listened to the sounds coming from the bathroom, where, as he always did on Sunday afternoon, Meyer, or maybe Götz, was splashing in a tub full of bubbles. He always took a long time to bathe, was capable of playing with yellow duckies and a little red boat for hours, and later, without the slightest compunction, stroll buck naked around the flat looking for his clothes. Götz, or Meyer, was full of gratitude for the organizational capabilities of Untersturmführer Andorfer, since, he said, it was no mean feat to meet all the conditions for the normal functioning of a camp. For instance, he said, you had to make sure that all the members of one family got onto the same transport, and that the number of staff in the kitchen diminished proportionately to the decreasing number of prisoners, that you held on as long as possible to the cobblers and locksmiths, and that you coordinated the number of block commanders and camp policemen, and that, most important, the camp administration functioned impeccably. Did I have any idea, I was asked by Götz, or perhaps it was Meyer, how much effort was needed to coordinate all of that? I wonder, said Götz, or Meyer, does that man ever have time to sleep? There must be writing and erasing to be done, he went on, you couldn't just write any old thing, there were essential acrobatics and somersaults and who knows what all, endless patience, for instance, let alone love for one's work, and he had to have some sort of schematic plan, something like that web you have up there in the frame on the wall. He stopped, looking over at my family tree. Hey, he asked finally, what do all these people mean to you? I didn't know what to say to him. I didn't exactly know where Meyer, or was it Götz, was, had he gone out, by chance? If the postman ran into him, he would not fare well. And Commander Andorfer certainly had his hands full. The camp emptied quickly, he had to prepare his final accounting, determine the state of the supplies, draw up an inventory, make a list of essential repairs, run through his final checklist, and with all that goes a certain emotional tension, a feeling of rupture, a mild sort of grief, almost melancholy, that it was all over, with a dose of anxiety, of course, as to how it would be evaluated up there where things are evaluated. He wasn't thinking of Heaven, he had Berlin in mind. Of course there were additional distasteful details to deal with, especially when it turned out that even with two round trips daily of Götz and Meyer's truck, the camp was not emptying fast enough. Andorfer had to relent under pressure and reinstate the good old firing squad, which had an especially detrimental effect on Götz and Meyer, who saw this as belittling their efforts, as well as altogether underestimating the significance of scientific advancement. But little differences of opinion like that are possible in every job, and in such situations it is always a good idea to seek compromises rather than aggravate discord and weaken military and every other readiness. Whatever the case, on May 10, 1942, the last group of Jews was taken from the Fairgrounds camp, including the members of the Administration and their families, and what was left of the cooks, tradesmen, and doctors. Once they were gone, a feathery cloud of silence descended on the camp. It rolled sluggishly round the emptiness of absence, and like a sponge it absorbed the sounds that tried to hide in the vacated pavilions, in the straw crushed between the boards of the cots, in the grease lining the bottoms of the kitchen pots, in the papers tossed on the floor of the Central Tower, in the shoes that were never picked up after they'd been resoled. On the mounds between the third and fourth pavilions, spring had long since come, grass was beginning to sprout. There are no reliable witness statements on the subject, but that doesn't mean it didn't happen. There were six women left in the camp, non-Jews, whose husbands and families had been taken off on various transports. They wandered the empty expanses of the camp for a week in deafening silence, bumping into one another. Sometimes it is like that: space that grows is actually shrinking, and what you used to long for becomes what you most dread. I fled, but no matter how I tried, I couldn't get away from the cloud of silence that threatened to burst my eardrums. I hope, I told the woman at the Jewish Historical Museum, that one piece of the cloud, or maybe even a whole, tiny cloudlet, its close cousin, managed to reach Jajinci and the five, or seven, Serbian prisoners, and that it buffered, at least a little, the zing of the bullets that united them with those they had so devotedly sent to their last rest. That is the only consolation, I said, I could offer them. Yes, answered the woman, but history, unfortunately, is not meteorology. But the heart, I wanted to tell her, is a meteorologist. I didn't say anything, I went down to the center of town, to Terazije, hoping that the urban bustle would help me shake off the pain nesting in my ears. Then I assigned my students an essay on the theme "The Sound and the Fury." I attended basketball games, sat in smoke-filled halls where people played bingo, drank beer in cafés where they were playing folk music. Nothing helped. Silence was crouching in my ear like a hermit crab in a snail shell, the way a crab carries its home across the ocean floor, the silence carried me deep under the surface of the world. The assessment of Jewish property began on December 9, 1941, when the first groups of Jews were sent to the Fairgrounds camp. And while frantic women and sobbing children got to know the inside of the pavilions that would be their homes for the next five months, though for some far fewer, the members of the commission for inventory and assessment of property compared their lists, rifled through boxes of keys, went into flats, measured and noted, underlined and collected. The flats and houses were already mute and cold, and like their owners they offered no resistance. It hurt them when the strange feet walked in, somewhere the parquet flooring creaked, somewhere the carpet moaned, but no one noticed. There were places where, in the vases and flowerpots, the flowers had wilted and gave off a sweetish smell. In the mirror you could still see the pale shadows of the people who used to live there. Full pans and unwashed coffeepots still sat on the stoves. Books crowded the shelves, in glassed-in cupboards holiday dishes shone, hats and kerchiefs hung from coatracks. The doormats, always the most loyal, tried to slip down the stairs at night and flee into the street. Because of that, I am convinced, because of the loyalty of things, sales went at a snail's pace, as it says in one book, and only ended in the autumn of 1943. The German authorities had lost patience long before and, in late summer 1942, handed all the Jewish property over to Serbia, receiving in return 360,000,000 dinars, which included compensation for damages to Germany during the war operations against Yugoslavia, as if the war had been fought only because of the Jews. And why was it that the war was fought? Götz and Meyer had no way of answering, and they looked at me as if I might answer their questions. I don't know anything, I told them. Götz and Meyer raised their index fingers simultaneously and admonished me. You know how to turn us into lighthouses, they shouted, but you don't know how to tell us over which shore or sea our light shines, how can that be? I replied that *sea* is too strong a word, that their light, a feeble light at best, was shining on a puddle, nothing more. I savored, no point in pretending I didn't, the wince of disgust flitting across the void of their faces. It seems to me, Götz, or Meyer, whispered to Meyer, or Götz, that he doesn't like us. Meyer, or maybe Götz, said nothing. He shoved his hands into his pocket, pulled out a paper bag, and offered me some chocolate. I put out my trembling fingers, ashamed of the loud gurgling sound that came from my stomach, took a chocolate, all dark and sticky, put it on my tongue, pushed it into my cheek, pressed it up against the roof of my mouth, and for an instant forgot everything, the cold and the hunger, the insomnia and the pain in my joints, the itching on my skin and scabs on my face, and I pranced around like a colt, like a kid, like a fawn, like all those animals in the picture books I had hidden under the straw bedding, and then I spread my arms and scampered back and forth, my knees high, making squeaky sounds and flying without a fumble into the spaces that opened up among people. Look at that kid, someone said, whizzing around like a plane. I opened my eyes. The wall clock was ticking softly, mutely, as if ashamed. Books were tossed around the room, files with photocopied documents, boxes of photographs, illustrated history books, statements from survivors, chronicles of war events, the memoirs of generals, diaries and letters. I didn't dare to move. I stood there and felt how I was retreating more and more into myself, drowning. I closed my eyes. No, no, Götz and Meyer said in unison, that won't help. I'd never seen them, I could only imagine them. There is no other way, said the rabbi at the funeral of my senile cousin, except the way that leads straight to the heart and then, purified, springs from the heart. If only I knew where the heart is, I mused, everything would be simpler. I packed up and went off to a village called S—. No one remembered the thin woman with the little boy. They remembered a tall woman with a chubby little girl and a man with a mustache who told fantastic stories about distant cities. I went from house to house and stared at the chickens, but not a single one showed the slightest inclination to approach my open hand. I spent the night in an unpainted house in a room on the first floor, on a sofa bed that no one had slept on before me. In the morning I spread *kajmak* cheese on a thick slice of bread and stepped into the dewy grass. Birds chirped in a little glade of trees up on the hill. I knew nothing about birds. It could have been a pygmy owl or a nutcracker, an oriole or a goldfinch, a thrush or a nightingale. You can't tell? asked Götz and Meyer. Disgraceful! They said those words as clearly as if they were standing right there. I spun round. A dog was sitting on the threshold. Mother never let us keep animals in our flat. Father fought for an aquarium with tropical fish, but the condition was that, no matter what, there could be no more than five fish in it. More than five, Mother said, is a horde, not a school, of fish. I closed my eyes again. Then I raised my arm and, without looking, started walking. Back when I was a boy, I liked to close my eyes, said Götz, or possibly Meyer, and how wonderful, the world looked so much nicer that way. I was the one who was supposed to say that, not Götz, or possibly Meyer, impersonal creations that they were, though I can no longer say things in my own voice with any certainty. I tried to picture how the three of us looked as we sat on a bench in the park, Götz, or Meyer, to my right and Meyer, or Götz, to my left. Their faces empty, shadows moving across my face. At night, when I dream them, we hold hands. In the morning, when I get up, I rinse my hands for ages under cold water, scrub them with a small, bristly brush, rub them until the skin complains. I bring them carefully to my nose, as if I'm holding a crystal bowl. I see that someone is watching me from the mirror, but I pretend not to notice. My life, I say aloud in the middle of a lecture on romanticism, is like a memory that doesn't know who is remembering it. The students look up, watch me, unblinking, briefly startled, then they shrug and quickly note down my words. If Götz and Meyer were to knock at your door tomorrow, I continue, what would you do? The students put down their pencils, look at each other, whisper. Who are Götz and Meyer, one girl finally asks, I mean, what did they write? They, I say, made pure poetry out of bodies. In rhymed verse? The question comes from the second row. In free verse, I respond, with a great deal of repetition. That means, says a boy from the first row, that they were before their time? I'd rather put it, I say, that they were outside time or, even better, that they did all they could to make time stand still. I confused them, no one dared complain. Just in case, I touched my left earlobe. That reassured them. It reassured me. I am dangling from my earlobe like an earring, I am swaying like a pendulum, fluttering like a buttercup in a crack in a concrete path. The path leads nowhere, it ends, you might say, before it begins. Sir, says that first girl, I don't get how this Götz and Meyer wrote poems in tandem, I always thought poetry comes out of solitude, inspiration, I don't know, arrives from afar, and speaks with a language that is understandable, I guess, to one person alone, and then that one person translates it, right?, into language all of us can understand. There is one thing you must understand when we are talking about Götz and Meyer, I say and release my earlobe. It seemed, I continue, as if there were two of them, but if you got under the skin a little, you would quickly have seen that the two were one and the same person. Hey, shouts a young man with a ponytail, like in that movie! He doesn't say which, but I know what they watch, I can picture this product of futuristic genetics. Precisely, I say, as if they had been painted by the same brush, and furthermore, then there was an entire army of people who were all the same. And all of them, the girl asked, wrote poems? They never stopped, I say. My earlobe is burning, warning me, but there is no turning back. Allow me, I say, to recite one of their poems to you. I feel the students' attention growing denser around me. I cough and say: Daniel, Isak, Jakov; Bukica, Estera, Sara; Solomon, Rafael, Haim; Rašela, Rifka, Klara. The class erupted in peals of laughter. I laughed with them, because only when I do that, opening my mouth wide and squeezing my eyes shut, can I hide the tears. Did Götz and Meyer ever burst into tears, except when they watched sappy romances in cinemas about poor girls falling into the hands of unscrupulous and ruthless capitalists? Tears are the most ordinary of excretions, Götz, or Meyer, said, while driving to Belgrade. They talked about all manner of things, it was a long trip, and so it was that they came to the subject of tears. I despise people who cry, said Meyer, or possibly Götz. Yes, replied Götz, or Meyer, real men never cry. Although, he said, growing solemn, I did cry when my aunt died. That doesn't count, Meyer, or Götz, consoled him. I was sorry for her cat, said Götz, or Meyer, it meowed so sadly as we lowered my aunt into her coffin. He bowed his head and pressed the corner of his eyes with his thumb and index finger, but when Meyer, or Götz, glanced over at him, he put it down to the grime. There certainly was grime, it's not that there wasn't, they could feel it between their teeth, touch it in their hair, even in their eyebrows, let alone on their uniforms. Every job has its downside, such is the order of things in the universe, and there is no point trying to change that. Take that brush and use it, Götz, or Meyer, must have told Meyer, or Götz, a thousand times if he'd told him once. If he'd been a pilot, which he had always wished he could be, at least he wouldn't have had to worry about the grime. But the uniform is the pride of every SS officer, and clothing, despite that old saying, does, after all, make the man, and Meyer, or possibly Götz, dedicated himself assiduously to cleaning. That was why, after all, task forces always ordered their victims to strip before they were shot. Naked, they were no longer people, which had an auspicious effect on the firing squad, because it is always easier to kill people who are nothing. And besides, naked people don't run away, mostly they try to shield their genitals and stand still, finding their last defense in a feeling of shame. The people who went into the "soul-swallower" still wearing their clothing at least weren't shamed, and that is some sort of comfort, isn't it? There is no comfort in death, the woman I met at the Jewish Historical Museum said, especially not in a death that someone else chooses for you. I wasn't thinking of them, I shouted, but of myself, because those small consolations are the only weapon with which I can stand up to the meaningless and horrible void filling the faces of Götz and Meyer, and without them, without those small consolations, I would sink right to the bottom, I would accept that what happens represents an implacable order of things and not some monstrous distortion, that human dignity is an illusion, that nothing exists except the dark face of evil, which each of us carries within, some people have it closer to the surface of their being, some in their depths, and actually, it isn't that we resist the repetition of evil, rather that sooner or later we recognize it in ourselves, joining with it in the end. I stopped talking, out of breath. I was always exhausted by long sentences, especially those that could have been said with fewer words, and even more by those that could have not been said at all. I never learned the lesson from that ancient saying that silence is a wall around wisdom. I talk until my mouth hurts, until my throat gets dry, until my larynx gets tied up in knots, as if words mean something, as if I could really save someone. Like a man who, lost in a forest, walks round in circles and keeps coming back to the place he started from, I keep starting from the beginning, closing my eyes to the failure of all my attempts. So I sat down, as if nothing had happened, and started writing letters to the military archives in Germany and Austria, to the documentation centers in Israel and America, even to Riga and Moscow, anywhere where there was the slightest possibility that I might stumble onto some trace. It is impossible, I figured, that Götz and Meyer vanished as if the earth had swallowed them up, although, in fact, it was easiest to imagine that off in the grass, by some road somewhere, their bones were rotting in an unmarked grave. In a couple of unmarked graves. No matter how odd it may sound, I did not wish for their death, rather I longed desperately for their life. I wanted to meet them, lively or decrepit old men, I wanted their faces to fill slowly with wrinkles or moles, see their teeth or hear the clacking of their dentures, sit with them on a bench in front of a house in a village or at the dining-room table in some old people's home, to hear the air wheezing in their lungs, how their hearts beat and guts growled, to watch them leaning on sticks, blinking at the glaring neon light, the spittle pooling in the corners of their mouths. I wouldn't ask them anything. I'd just sit there next to them and be quiet, and let my quiet wash over them. And then, when there was nothing left in them but that quiet, when they were swimming in it like fish in the sea, I wanted them to turn to me, and in their eyes, which had finally filled with color, blue or brown, I would be able to see that they knew who I was though they had never seen me, and they would know that they had lost the chance to know me, I wanted to see them remember. At that point I could get up and go, but I'd stay a little longer. I would sit next to them and watch the sun set behind the hill and the shadows moving toward us with giant steps. That is that: that is the end of the road. In reality, however, the end of the road was nowhere in sight. The answers I received brought me no closer. They led me to the vast expanses of the Soviet Union, described camps and ghettoes in Poland, listed data on the killing of ailing Jewish children in Kislovodsk, listed names that meant nothing to me. In May 1942, Untersturmführer Dr. August Becker visited, on assignment, several places where gas trucks had been used, with the objective of ascertaining their efficiency and proposing further guidelines. In his final report he mentioned two problems: the great mental pressure on the members of the SS who unloaded the trucks themselves, because they did not wish to entrust this job to prisoners who were prepared to take every available opportunity to escape, as well as a second problem, the frequent breakdowns resulting from the poor condition of Soviet roads. There is nothing to suggest that Dr. Becker came to Belgrade. Had he done that, I don't doubt that Götz and Meyer would have agreed with his second conclusion, keeping in mind the problem with the rear axle on their Saurer. However, in the case of the first problem, they could point to what had clearly been successful cooperation with the prisoners, who not only unloaded the trucks but buried the corpses, which had an exceptionally salutary effect on the German soldiers, so that during the work you could often hear their cheery banter; for all that, it was enough to promise the prisoners some sort of reward, in this case they were promised that when they had completed their work, they would be sent to a work camp in Norway. Götz and Meyer, of course, were not the masterminds behind this successful organizational structure, they would not want him to think they were taking credit for someone else's accomplishments, far from it. They don't know who deserves the credit, perhaps Commander Andorfer, but whoever came up with the idea showed that, with a little self-confidence, one can overcome problems that seem, at first, to be insoluble. Fine lads, Götz and Meyer, aren't they now? Under other conditions, considering how diligent they were, surely they would have headed up a labor union. But, had he heard their testimony, Dr. Becker would not have hesitated: gas trucks were good, especially when dealing with the smaller, more distant Jewish communities, but their effect was not sufficient for places with a larger concentration of Jews, where – again I reach for my calculator – the cost of maintaining a camp with stationary gas chambers and crematoria, with the use of a free labor force, was far cheaper than the cost of using the gas trucks and the extremely awkward involvement of military troops, who could be used to greater benefit elsewhere. In short, Götz and Meyer lost their job at some point. The gas trucks died out like dinosaurs. Making way for more perfect forms, camps functioning as death factories. Science must move forward, there can be no mercy here. Perhaps there were certain sentimental recollections, a tenderness stirred by the sentence: Do you remember those good old Saurers? But that would have been all, no trace of mercy, science has no time for such emotions, no time for any emotion, especially when such a vital task is involved. Eh, Götz and Meyer gestured dismissively, if we had been caught up in thinking like that, we never would have done anything. They are conscientious, they always arrive on time, they are calm and cheerful, their signatures are legible, their uniforms tidy, their step light. Nothing can be held against them. And then when Götz, or was it Meyer, walks into the camp and begins handing out chocolates! At times like that, Meyer, or was it Götz, who simply didn't like children much, still was stabbed by jealousy now and again. That's nice, he'd think, when you are liked for the work you do, but still he couldn't make himself behave the way Götz, or maybe Meyer, did. Those revolting little creeps, what is there to talk about with them, he wouldn't have put his hand on their heads, and look how skinny they are, and some of them with those bulging bellies, with those sunken, black-ringed eyes. Horrible. Though, interestingly, Meyer, or Götz, was not particularly convinced of Götz's, or Meyer's, sincerity in his expressions of concern for those kids. I have a feeling, says Meyer, or Götz, that this was all an agreement, probably with Commander Andorfer – who had already managed to come up with the rules for the non-existing camp, why shouldn't he think up the chocolates – and once, while we were in Jajinci waiting for the unloading to finish, the two of them talked a little way off from the truck, and I saw how Commander Andorfer handed him something white, which I later saw quite clearly was a paper bag of chocolates. A brown-noser's words if ever I heard them, wholly unbefitting an SS-Scharführer, but people are fragile, there is no human being who, sooner or later, won't crack. Look at me: I am lying on the floor like a whipped dog, I've rested my head on a pile of books, I'm staring at an empty wall. I am lying, pressed down by figures, scenes from photographs, descriptions, technical details on the production of trucks, numbers, averages, names. I have a feeling I'll be paralyzed forever. I will never be able to go out again. Götz and Meyer's warnings that only the weak of spirit fall don't help. This is not news to me. How many times have I collapsed under heaps of notebooks containing homework assignments, and how I'd really collapse once I had finished marking! And the other day, while I was climbing up Rhigas Pheraios Street, I felt something touch me when I was standing on a corner. I don't know if I'll be able to describe that touch. Like the impression of a moist palm on your face. It doesn't matter. I stood there on that corner, facing a building, convinced that one of my relatives must once have lived there. No need to look down the lists in my bag and check the address. Or perhaps it was that Götz and Meyer's truck had passed this way, maybe that was what held me, and I imagined how one of them might draw the other's attention to the balding man standing on the corner, gesticulating and talking to himself. At the Library of the Municipality of Belgrade, they even warned me that they'd throw me out if I didn't stop bothering the other users with my mumbling. Götz, or Meyer, one of them, also liked to talk to himself from time to time, especially when they were driving through monotonous scenery. Meyer, or Götz, was irritated at first by the tiresome drone of the two identical voices, but later, when he got used to their noise, they started making him drowsy. He would stare out of the window, his eyes closing, and then he squinted through his lashes, and then he dropped off to sleep. He dozed like a baby, with a smile on his lips, his eyelids fluttering, his cheeks dimpling. Only a peaceful man, pleased with his life, who feels fulfilled, can sleep like that. What I'd give to be in his place! When I wake up in the morning, the sheet is wound round my throat, the duvet is on the floor, my hands are twisted up in the pillowcase. I could talk for hours of my dreams – more wrestling matches than dreams. I dreamed, for instance, how I was wandering through the labyrinth of the family tree; I was wandering for ages, my feet hurt; finally I caught sight of a way out and gladly ran toward it and found myself at the gate to the pavilion at the Fairgrounds, choked by the stench of fear and desperation; I feel nausea rising and try to hide, crouching in a corner, but no matter how I try, I can't regurgitate anything; then in the distance I catch sight of Götz and Meyer wearing white hospital gowns; with their arms outstretched, faceless, walking toward me. Dreams like that make my face clench up. Sometimes I have to press my face with my fingers to push the wrinkles up off my forehead, stretch my eyelids. At school, in the classroom, I don't dare look up at the students. My head bowed, poring over an open folder, I listen to them discussing novels written on subjects from World War II. As if you were living in a war, I tell them, talk about it that way, as if you were in a war now. Götz and Meyer are sitting in the last row, whispering, ripping pages out of their notebooks and folding paper airplanes. Later, at break, they eat hot dogs with mustard in a nearby park. Through the window of the classroom, hunched behind the curtains, I watch as bits of bread vanish into their facial voids. In twosomes like that, usually one is tall and the other short, one chubby, the other slender, but there is practically no difference between Götz and Meyer: they are the same height, of ordinary build, they wear the same size boots. Fine, one of them has slightly wider feet than the other, which means that his boots chafe him a little more, but a little difference like that, or so they say, only emphasizes their similarity, their walk, for instance, or the way they raise their hand in greeting. Götz actually could be Meyer, and Meyer, indeed, could be Götz. Maybe they are, who knows? Both talk with equal earnestness about their Saurer, praising it with carefully chosen words, without hesitating to make certain comments, for instance: on the instability of the truck's body when it was filled to capacity, which meant that it was essential to cut back on the number of items in each load, which had as a consequence an increased consumption of fuel, because the carbon monoxide had to fill more empty space. The smaller the body of the truck, they concluded, the greater its effect. Later, in a book, I happened upon a German report from June 1942 that discusses in almost the same words the problem of the stability of gas trucks. The author's position, which Götz and Meyer couldn't have known, is quoted: had they reduced its size, they would have thrown the balance of the entire truck out of kilter, and then the front axle would have had to bear an incomparably greater pressure. In practice, however, those who submitted the report claimed, the load would rush instinctively to the back door as it closed, and at the end of the trip, the greatest number of them would be right there, which meant that the weight of the load was heavily over the rear axle, thereby maintaining the necessary equilibrium. This same document is touching in its concern for the welfare of the load, which found itself in the dark in the back of the truck, screaming and banging at the door, and therefore it would be better, the document proposes, that there be a light in the truck at the very beginning when the load is being processed, which would help to reassure the load itself, and, I conclude, ensure a more equally distributed inhalation of the carbon monoxide. The author also remarks that it would be necessary to secure the lightbulb with metal netting, probably so that no one would break it and, God forbid, cut their hand or get an electric shock. Götz and Meyer would most certainly have supported such a suggestion, though they doubt that this would entirely do away with the screams and howls, because in their case, where the loading proceeded in perfect order, sooner or later, especially after they had stopped and hooked up the exhaust pipe, someone would start to shout, and the rest would join in. In the end, it never lasted very long, and soon the shouting, as their experience showed, turned into those sounds you hear when you can't hear them anymore. It is over, Götz, or Meyer, would say, the one who is definitely married. He said it every day, sometimes even twice, and Meyer, or Götz, the one who isn't, maybe, married, would always wince. There is no mention of this in their reports, which I never saw, but I reckon that Götz and Meyer had to have written at least one report. I like to picture them bent over sheets of paper, frowning and chewing on a pencil. They turn to me: Why aren't you helping us now? No one can help history, the woman at the

Museum says. She says this with such certainty that I don't even try to respond. While I sit across from her, I know how my students feel. Then I got a letter from Vienna confirming how after the war there was no investigation in Germany into the case of Götz and Meyer, and that there is no way to find out what happened to them. I read the letter in front of the letter boxes. I paid no attention to the stamp. My knees shook, and I had to sit down on the stairs. I didn't sit long, something nudged me in the back, I barely managed to grab my belongings, get in the line behind the others, while bits of sentences were coming through from all sides, deep sighs, choked-back sobs. We climbed into the military truck, and through a hole in the tarpaulin, while we were driving, I saw how the buildings and streets passed, and then we reached the bridge, and Belgrade faded into the distance. Picture the life collected in a grain of sand, I told my students. Yesterday it was an entire world, today it is a dot. It is impossible to describe, because in doing so you'd be doing an injustice either to the world or to the dot. You can't talk, you see, of both in the same language; one starts where the other lets off; one cannot grasp the other. This is far too convoluted for them: I see their eyebrows furrow, their lips purse. Life is history, I write on the board, and in history no one can help anyone else. Strange, but when he arrived at the Fairgrounds camp and took the bag of chocolates out of his pocket, Götz, or Meyer, felt as if he was leaving history behind. He moved through space outside time, existing only in a present belonging to no one. Then he'd blink, and the next moment he'd find himself behind the wheel of the Saurer, whistling a march, pleased that it is not his turn to sit in the passenger seat, to be in charge of reattaching the exhaust pipe. Although he was not superstitious, he'd feel something evil in the air when he got out of the truck, and suddenly, while motes of dust were falling on his uniform, he heard the noise and cries coming from the back of the truck. Once he heard bees buzz, another time a bird sang, but the dull noise grew, especially once he came closer to the underside of the truck with the exhaust pipe in his hand. In one of those dreams when Meyer, or Götz, had to wake him, with threats that the next time he'd pour a glass of water down his neck, which he never did, in one of those dreams, he dreamed someone spoke his name through that little hole. Enunciated it loud and clear: Wilhelm Götz. And then said: You are Erwin Meyer. What a terrible dream, even now he cringed when he remembered it. He had never told it to anyone, although once he had barely kept himself from telling it when he was with Untersturmführer Andorfer. While they were smoking a little way off from the truck, waiting for the unloading to finish, they talked about dreams, and when Andorfer told him of his own exciting dream, something about a double-headed eagle, he wanted to tell him his, but then he bit his tongue, coughed, and said he had a sore throat. Andorfer put his hand in his pocket and pulled out a bag of cough drops. He wasn't fond of the taste of menthol, though his love of chocolate was famous, but he accepted the offer and put the lozenge on his tongue. The children at the camp took his candy in just the same way: they put them on their tongue and then, eyes closed, pressed them up against the roofs of their mouths. There were children, especially among the youngest of them, who took the chocolates with their grimy fingers and with careful nibbles bit off all the chocolate coating. Then with their little tongues they poked around in the filling as if seeking buried treasure. It occurs to me that none of them knew what Götz's, or Meyer's, names were. They'd cluster around him and shout: Mister, over here, Mister! And not only the children, none of the prisoners at the camp had any idea what Götz and Meyer were really called, though it is easy to imagine that they referred to them somehow, maybe as Slim, or Whiskers, in a word, with whatever made Götz, Götz and Meyer, Meyer. They knew, I am thinking here of the prisoners, things that elude me, while I know what eludes them: I know Götz's and Meyer's names, and the real purpose of the Saurer, and the real meaning of the words *transport* and *load*, and the story about the fabled camp in Romania, or Poland. Although when Götz and Meyer are at issue, I must admit I do not know who is who, which makes me, in a sense, more ignorant than those who knew nothing of their names. I keep on about names, as if they meant something, but in fact, I may have already said this, they are empty shells, shed skins, except that a shell, when you put it to your ear, murmurs like the sea, while nothing can be heard from their names but silence. I can't listen to silence anymore. Not long ago, about 3:00 in the afternoon, when the rush hour is at its worst, I walked for a long time around the streets, went to the houses where my relatives used to live, and then I tried to determine which route each of them took that December morning when they went to the headquarters of the Special Police for Jews. They were bent over, lugging their bundles, dragging suitcases along the pavement, checking to see they'd locked the door and watered the plants. Someone said that he couldn't remember when he'd been up this early, but he didn't regret it, the morning air was so pleasant. The air around me, at that very moment, was extremely unpleasant. I walked through the streets that Götz and Meyer's Saurer had passed through. I was on the corner where something had touched me once, but I didn't feel anything this time. Maybe in the meanwhile, in the time between my two visits to that imagined history, my relatives had moved? I will have to check that in the lists. I refer to lists, but in fact this is a vast documentation, in countless files with headings and a variety of symbols directing you to other files with related material, which allowed me to put my hand quickly on all the documents relevant to any person or event. Every one of my relatives or, more precisely, every family had its own file, as did Commander Andorfer, the Jewish hospital, the Gestapo, the Department for Social Welfare and Social Institutions, Jajinci. Götz and Meyer, too, had their file, but in it were just copies of the telegrams announcing their arrival and departure. The instructions on their file cover direct you to the following files: Saurer – technical equipment; Saurer – application, maps; Commander Andorfer, Untersturmführer; Riga; Correspondence – Austria; Correspondence – Germany; the Fairgrounds; a file with my name on it. Götz and Meyer are mentioned here and there in these files, but altogether there was barely enough to fill a page. Their faces continued to be white splotches, resembling flags of surrender, which was altogether the wrong impression, because if there was anyone in need of hanging out that sort of flag, it was I, not Götz and Meyer. Several times I was, indeed, tempted to surrender, I was barely able to restrain myself from doing so, as I was lost in the labyrinth of the family tree or among the papers thrown on the floor of my room. I, too, have had times when I have felt like giving up, said Götz, or maybe it was Meyer, the monotony of the work was killing me, the endless repetition, one day at the wheel, the next day responsible for the exhaust pipe, and then over again, as if there were nothing else left in life. The other, Meyer, or Götz, made no effort to conceal his disagreement. Exactly, he said, this is our life as long as the task we have been assigned to exists. He had long been suspicious of his fellow officer's genuine devotion to the ideals of the Reich. His work effort was not being questioned, there could be no doubt about it, just as there could be no question of his loyalty, but there was something too tender in him, yes, it radiated from his melancholy, along with something else he couldn't put his finger on, but he was certain that the key to the door to the other side was right here. He couldn't say exactly what that other side was, this was something he still had to discover, but it was enough to open all four eyes and listen to the night voices from the adjacent bed. If I had known that, Götz, or was it Meyer, the first one, told me in confidence, I would have treated him differently. There you go: you open your heart to people and they hold their noses. I hadn't understood what he was trying to say, but I had no will to pursue it. I felt uncomfortable while I sat with them under the Sava Bridge and drank beer. The beer dulled me, the heat reached us despite the shade and the river, the pavilions at the Fairgrounds were at my back, or at the back of my neck. Here, not far from us, prisoners were carrying their dead over the ice-shackled river. They must have seemed like black dots to someone looking down at them from the Kalemegdan fortress in the center of Belgrade. They moved so slowly, it took them so long to get across, that an observer had to take his gloves off from time to time and rub his eyes. The cold nipped at their faces, tightened the skin on their chins, gnawed at their ears. The ground slipped under them at every step, but still the prisoners had a firm hold on the corpses, as if there were something that might happen to them if the corpses fell from their hands and slid onto the ice. No one dies twice, said Götz, or Meyer, and burped. He couldn't know that, two years after their stay in Belgrade, the German Occupation forces decided to burn the corpses they had buried at Jajinci. So my relatives did die twice after all, once in the darkness of the back of the truck, aching for fresh air, and a second time on a heap of bodies, aching to rest in peace. As they were disinterred, a witness states, valuables were stripped from the corpses: rings, watches, chains, gold teeth. After the corpses had been burned, the ashes were sifted in case any objects of precious metal had been missed. That covered the cost, I reckon, of the disinterment, and there must have been a little extra left over. The things that were collected were sent to Berlin in the end, and Götz, or Meyer, and I kept sitting there under the bridge, drinking warm beer. I asked him whether he knew how long fish live. It suddenly occurred to me that in the Sava maybe there still is a fish alive who was swimming around under the ice at the time and saw the shadowy figures walking so carefully with their heavy loads. Götz, or Meyer, described a circle over his forehead with the neck of the beer bottle which might have meant he thought I'd gone clean out of my mind. This is not far from the truth. Anyone else in my place would have been worried, even seen a doctor, there are various places a person can go to get advice, but I keep clenching my teeth and going on as if nothing had happened. Sometimes you win when you admit defeat, but not with me. I would rather tilt at windmills, even the old and decrepit kind, the way they are now, Götz and Meyer, if they are alive. I never met them, I can only imagine them. I'm back where I began. This is what my life has turned into: stumbling, looking back, starting anew. One of those three lives I was living in parallel, maybe even a fourth. The rest continued to follow me, unchanged, and I'd wake up like Götz, or Meyer, eager to work, and go to sleep like a thirteen-year-old boy preparing for his bar mitzvah and repeating words in a language that made his throat ache. None of my relatives in the camp could be described as a thirteen-year-old boy, nor do I know where he came from, nor which life he belongs to. Götz and Meyer are also unable to help me. If we had remembered all those faces, they say, we'd remember nothing else. The boy kept popping up, and on one occasion, instead of my own hands, I saw his, clear as day. He was clutching a mug of milk and he was thirsty. He was in me that day, when, in a voice squeaky with excitement, I proposed to my students that we spend our next class in a hands-on demonstration. Although beside themselves at the thought that they wouldn't have to be in school, they wanted to know what was going to happen. The boy had, in the meanwhile, faded, leaving me to respond. It was going to be about the difference between the tangible world and art, I explained, but also about the similarity between an instant of reality and a figment of the imagination. I was pretty busy for a few days. I had to find a school bus, collect money from the students, work out the route, get my thoughts together. This last item was the hardest for me, I admit. Then on the family tree, in a forgotten corner, I found a distant relative, a Matilda, who had died in 1929. I never learned anything about her, as if she were cloaked in a family secret. I couldn't find her grave in the Jewish cemetery, even in the overgrown Ashkenazi section. Because of her I went to see the Jewish cemetery in Zemun, although none of my relatives ever lived in Zemun, with the exception, of course, of those months they spent at the Fairgrounds camp. And so, taking care that Götz and Meyer didn't notice, I explained to myself that poor Matilda must have died in childbirth. The boy who was born then, who had been dragging the prickly Hebrew words out of my throat, came from her extramarital affair with a man whom she never betrayed. The boy was given the name Adam, and Matilda, as if her death were not enough, was dropped into the deep well of forgetting. Her photographs were ripped up, her old school books burned, her clothing given to charitable organizations. How it happened that Adam was never entered onto the lists of Belgrade Jews, I'll never know, but his name was not on the summonses distributed in December 1941. Despite that, and despite the advice of the aunt whose home he lived in then, Adam packed his little suitcase on the evening of December 7, before he went to bed. Along with some underwear and a warm blue sweater, he packed the white shirt and black pants that had been set aside for his bar mitzvah, and two apples that he took from the cupboard in the kitchen. One of these would be filched by an unknown boy who would threaten to beat him if he cried. He didn't cry. I told all this to the students while we drove around town on the bus. I spoke over the driver's sound system. I held the microphone in my right hand, and I clutched my notes in my left. There was nothing in the notes I didn't already know by heart, I just needed them there as encouragement. The faith in paper is odd, as if history were no more than a trace of ink, as if paper were more enduring than everything else. I clutched that wad of paper like a thief snatching a squash from a field, claiming that all he was trying to do was find shelter from the wind. I stood there, arms akimbo, to keep my balance as the bus rocked like a boat, which I referred to as Noah's Ark. If there was a wind blowing, I didn't feel it. While I was speaking, the driver hummed a melody to himself so at the moment when the boy walks with his aunt toward the truck, I had to ask him to stop. He did so, reluctantly, but he whistled a bit from time to time after that. Not all drivers are like Götz and Meyer, I have to say. They always knew when it was time for a song, for whistling, for yodeling, and it was duty first, and an order, even when expressed as a request, had to be respected. This is where it all began, I said as we got to George Washington Street where the Special Police for Jews were stationed although it might be better to say, I added, that everything ended here. And, of course, I continued, now it is clear and sunny, but you have to picture the December gloom, a chill morning, shivers that engulf the entire body. They had locked the front door for the last time, picked up their suitcases, and set out. Adam stood and watched as his aunt turned the key in the lock and pressed the door handle and then, as she was leaving, straightened the skewed mat. They must have had at least an inkling, like all the rest, that they would never be back, and that they probably were setting out on the road their husbands and fathers had already taken, but they struggled with it, as you could see in the way they walked, interrupted by quick shudders, brief flights from the truth. They themselves fled, hoping that they would arrive where they were headed as someone else, that they could go back to their flowers in their pots on their windowsills while that other person kept walking toward the building housing the Special Police. Only Adam was there, heart and soul, because even if he had wanted to, he had no one to flee to, nowhere to go back to. He held his little suitcase, ready, at last, to set out into the world. The driver whistled softly between clenched teeth. His whistling was closer to hissing, but I recognized the tune. Now I'd like to know, I said into the microphone, what would you have done in his place. Silence washed over the bus like water dumped from a basin. Even the driver turned. I waited. First a girl with long blond hair spoke. She pushed her fringe out of her eyes and said that she would take her hamster with her, that she couldn't bear the thought of little Ćira, which must have been the hamster's name, staying behind without her. My life without Ćira, she added, would be nothing. The rest all spoke at once. Apparently my students owned an entire zoo, and they would not leave their homes if they had to go without their dogs, cats, parakeets, canaries, turtles, rabbits, ant colonies, praying mantises. The boy with a ponytail was the one who had the praying mantises; he kept them in jars and sometimes let them fight. Even the driver piped up: he kept pigeons. I'm sorry, I said, but the instructions are clear and allow only clothing, bedding, dry food for three days, that sort of thing. Why, this is inhuman, exclaimed the blond girl. This time she didn't brush her fringe aside, and her eyes flashed angrily behind her hair. If we keep this up, I thought, they'll report me to the Society for Protection of Animals, but aloud I said: That is the difference I want to talk about, the fact that you keep imagining reality as if it were an artwork in which you have a choice, while in the tangible world there is no choice, you have to participate, you cannot step out of what is going on and into something else, there is nothing else except what is going on, whether you like it or not, and that means you must feel the cold taking over, and you must have at least an inkling that you will never be back, and that you will never see your pets again, and that your rooms, as you left them, will soon be entered by people for whom none of your mementos, none of those little things you fuss over, will mean anything. The blond girl began to cry. She sobbed and sniffled, and wiped her tears away with her arm. Adam, however, did not cry. He climbed up into the military truck, sat down on the wooden floor, hugged his suitcase. Around him women and other children crowded in, and in that jostling, surrounded by excited voices, he felt a certainty he had never known before. He wanted the truck to leave soon, and the ride to last long. The truck did leave soon, I told them, though the drive did not last as long as Adam hoped it would. Through a gap in the tarpaulin, Adam saw people in a line, then the buildings began to move by faster and faster. The driver nodded, turned his key, shifted gears, pressed the accelerator. The blond girl had stopped crying. She was staring at the floor and, if I saw rightly, was chewing her lower lip. I should have given her a hand-kerchief, now it was too late. I spread my feet farther to keep my balance, but no matter how I tried, I couldn't stop swaying, as if I were inching along high above them on a loosely strung wire. The route we are taking, I said into the microphone, is not, of course, the route they took, but the final result is the same: after the city comes the bridge, after the slopes and cliffs stretch the plains. They say, I went on, that plains are soothing, and there is truth in that, though this holds more for those who live there than those who carry at least a hint of uneven terrain in their feet. They, like all sailors on dry ground, do not know how to walk through these peaceful expanses, and they tend to trip even when there are no obstacles to trip over. Turn round, I said when the bus got to the bridge, and look at how the city is getting farther behind us and closing up at the same time, and how although it hasn't budged from where it was, it seems to be fading. All the students turned and peered over the backs of their seats, even the driver glanced into his rearview mirror several times. You might talk about that as a physical pain, I said, as if someone were tearing patches of skin from your body. I heard several gasps, but no one turned back to me. They stared at Belgrade as if it would disappear any minute. Only Adam remained quiet, crouched in his corner, unmoved by the general excitement, sighs, and sobs. If he felt anything, it was excitement at the prospect of a journey, he had never traveled anywhere before, with a suitcase no less, and he started thinking of the books he had read, *Children of Captain Grant* and *In Desert and Wilderness*. He had even started writing a story not long ago about a boy, a stowaway on a boat that sank somewhere in the Atlantic Ocean. He got off with a few of the sailors, in a boat that had no oars, no food or water, and here he stopped, and couldn't figure out where to take the story next. The river they were crossing, of course, didn't much resemble an ocean, but water is water, isn't it? Everyone agreed. Some things are simply accepted without the need for a lot of convincing. When the truck crossed over to the other shore, Adam thought of a huge city, entirely of glass, in which you could see the endless blue of the sky. The reality, of course, at the Fairgrounds was something else entirely, but no less exciting than the one the thirteen-year-old boy was imagining. He got up early in the morning, shivered during roll call, tasted the watery soup, watched them carrying away the dead, and yet at certain moments he couldn't repress the happiness he felt that he was experiencing it all. He knew that he was in the middle of the greatest adventure of his lifetime, and he did not want to miss a single part of it, although he was no different from that little boy in the boat who was dependent on the whims of the sea's currents. Adam didn't understand the currents that were sweeping him along, but he could sense their force, and he soon realized that there was no point in resisting. But what happened, asked a student in a checked shirt, to his prayers? I never mentioned prayers, I answered into the microphone, all I said was that he was preparing for his bar mitzvah, when he was to come of age in his faith. I did say that.

And he really had been working at it, I think, repeated to himself the part of the Five Books of Moses that you are supposed to read in Hebrew. I do not believe I convinced the student in the checked shirt. At that age, suspicion is a constant companion. On that point, of course, Götz and Meyer were not so different from them. They trusted only Germans, anyone else might cross over and join the enemy at any moment, if they hadn't already done so. They even cast suspicious glances at each other now and then. The enemy has been known to crop up in the most unexpected places. By this time we had arrived at the Fairgrounds. Before that, we passed a hotel and business premises entirely of glass, quite similar to those in Adam's fantasy, and which never would have occurred, for instance, to Götz and Meyer, although they drove their truck through this area countless times. They were thinking of other things: of where they were born – a place somewhere, I assume, deep in the German or Austrian Alps – but no need to rush things, the time would come for Götz and Meyer, indeed. First I told the students about how the camp was organized, no, first we walked around in silence, I allowed them to sense the space, I prepared them for what it used to look like, and only then did I begin to tell them about how the camp was organized, the accommodations, the daily schedule, the workshops, the living and the dead. They stood huddled in a circle around me, as if they were afraid to step back at all. They had already known, of course, that they were on a journey with no return, but hope kept them from truly believing that. There can be no doubt that the greenery contributed, the dense greenery that had surrounded the Fairgrounds on all sides, so that from far away a person would be convinced he was coming to a wooded area, and once he stepped into the tangle of shadows, he might think it was a park, rather overgrown, yet still a park. So I slowly erased it all, that greenery, removed it leaf by leaf, picked up every twig, until nothing was left but the bare, decrepit buildings, standing in a void. Nothing is more awful than a void, nothing more present than absence. After all, I told them, that was how Adam felt: he was here, but actually he wasn't, just as the camp, despite its overcrowding, consisted of an empty place in which every step echoed like the blow of a hammer on an anvil. Do you understand what I'm talking about? They didn't. They looked at me and blinked, the way people blink when they are startled by a gust of wind or the sun bursting through the clouds, and what would they do if I were to ask to hear how their teeth chatter, their stomachs growl, their joints creak? Adam heard all those things, from other people and from himself, especially at night, when he had to bite the pillow to stop his teeth from chattering and curl up in a ball to quiet the howling of his stomach. By day, he'd double over with a nasty cramp cinching his stomach in a steel vice, but even then he kept his eyes open, because someone had to see it all and remember every humiliation, every escape into madness and flight into dreams, every bit of frostbite or bruise from being struck by the butt of a gun or kicked by boots. But why, said a girl with spectacles, when, at the end, he would, I mean, since he knew, he had to know, that after everything else the only . . . She didn't finish her sentence. She couldn't say the word *die*, as if she would be taking her own life by saying it. Götz and Meyer would certainly have understood her: they didn't use the word either, instead they spoke of "moving" or "processing," using the euphemistic German terminology in which no things are what the language usually calls them but are something else, a reality taking place within unreal coordinates. Memory, I said, is the only way to conquer death, even when the body is forced to disappear, especially then, because the body merely goes the way of all matter and spins in an endless circle of transformations, while the spirit remains in a transparent cloud of mental energy moving slowly through the world and pouring, randomly as it first may seem, into restored matter, so that no one knows what they'll find in themselves when they look within. I stopped talking. If I had gone on, I surely would have lost them forever. I could see in their desperate glances, in their faces, which expressed a fear of slipping, the possibility that they might stay in a world about which they knew nothing until yesterday, until that very moment. I breathed deeply. That frightened them too, as if I were leaving them no oxygen, as if I were sucking up the last bit of air from their lungs. I smiled. Now we'll talk poetry, I said. Tell me how experience becomes a poem. For a moment their eyes flashed with the old fire, but it was already too late, they had gone out, those fires, as Adam's memories descended from the heavenly heights and sank into their every pore. By the way, no matter how odd it may sound, while he was at the camp Adam did write poetry. Not, indeed, on paper, because that would have been a luxury for frozen fingers, but in his head, especially in the morning, in line, during roll call, and in the evening, when the sun sank beyond the plains. They were short poems, with flawed verse schemes and failed rhymes, but they were poems, a series of images that expressed wonder at the miracle of creation and the insecurity of existence in a world in which there are no discernible shapes. You might say, I added, that those were prayers, they were so sincere and simple, so precise in expressing fervor, fear, and submission. If Götz and Meyer had had a chance to hear them, perhaps they would have been transformed and given up the task they'd been entrusted with or at least approached it with a feeling of alarm. You can't love God and act against his will at the same time. The moment I said those words, I realized how pointless it is to say such a thing, but the students believed me, I could see that in their lowered eyes, in the way their fingers were intertwined, the joints clutching so tightly that they were white. But, I said, this is a hands-on class, let's set our speculations and spiritual questions aside, and let's do something. I said this, in fact, more for my own sake than for theirs, just as I chastised myself when I'd get lost in guesswork standing in front of the drawing of my family tree that used to hang on the wall of my sitting room. I must say here that it is entirely possible in the case of Götz, or possibly Meyer, that God was more present than one usually thinks, because Götz, or possibly Meyer, survived the explosion of a bomb that killed at least nine soldiers from his company, thanks only, as he often said, to God's will, somewhere on the Eastern Front. Because of that Götz, or maybe Meyer, thanked the Lord every day for his goodness, especially while they were jouncing along in the truck on their way to Jajinci, while in the same truck, in the back, Jews were screaming at their God with their last breath, asking him why he wasn't there, why he wasn't there yet, why he was never there? There is nothing so awful as dying in doubt, coming unraveled, without anything to lean on. I stopped talking, again. I had said too much, as always. A breeze touched our foreheads, rustled the leaves, the sky glistened like gelatin. Suddenly, the bus driver appeared from behind the barracks. His eyes were bloodshot, his cheeks creased, he must have fallen asleep leaning on his hand or the wheel. How much longer is this going to take, he grumbled, we need to leave soon. A few more minutes, I said, Götz and Meyer are on their way, they haven't got here yet. The driver nodded, turned, scratched his rear end, and disappeared around the same corner. The students stared sadly after him, as if he were taking with him their last hope of salvation, which was not far from the truth. I recited the dimensions of the special vehicle that Götz and Meyer drove, the way I'd found them in a confidential report: 5,800 millimeters long, the height of the load space 1,700 millimeters, total structural weight 1,700 kilos, able to carry a load of up to 4,500 kilos. That meant, I said, that the vehicle could take about a hundred people who weighed up to 50 kilos each, which, after three months spent at the Fairgrounds camp, was a realistic average weight per prisoner. All the students looked reprovingly at a chubby girl who wore a headband, and a blush crept across her face. That also means, I added, that many had to bend down as they got in, and that later, during the ride, and especially after the light was put out, they bumped their heads on the ceiling as they tried to get as comfortable as possible. The people driving these vehicles, I continued, went through a special training course, and often among them, which may have been the case with Götz, or Meyer, or both, there were soldiers who had come back from the front because of injuries. At first, however, despite this training, certain mistakes were made that, fortunately, did not detract from the efficiency of the work, but did attract the attention of their superiors, so in Untersturmführer Dr. Becker's report, whose inspection trip I have already mentioned, I am sure that he draws attention to the necessity of gradually increasing the level of gas, because "it has been shown," I read from one of the sheets of paper in my bundle, "that by releasing the gas as regulated, death comes swiftly and the prisoners die half-asleep. Now you no longer see convulsed and disfigured faces on those who have been suffocated, and there is not as much vomiting and defecation as there used to be earlier, when the gas was released all at once." Their concern for the welfare of the prisoners is touching, I must say. I've said it before, I am repeating myself. Although I have no reliable information, I am convinced Götz and Meyer did not make that sort of mistake. I have not managed to track down any written complaints about their work. On the contrary, one might say, though there are no such expressions in military jargon, they fulfilled their assignment with a dedicated tenderness. I stood at the center of the ring of students. Götz and Meyer are still quite far away, but soon their truck will pull up at the gate to the camp, there, behind you. Again I dedicated myself to my bundle of papers. The tense breathing of my students and, if I am not mistaken, the occasional sob, made me feel as if I were amid a tossing ocean of air. I was both floating and sinking, like a divided being that cannot reconnect. An awkward feeling that sends chills down my spine even now. The list in my hand turned into a flapping sail. Each of you, I said, will now become someone else, each will become first the name, and then the person who bore that name. I began handing out names as if I were scattering seeds. The boys became my boy cousins, the girls my girl cousins. I gave them an age for each name, an occupation, real or imagined, sometimes hair color, density of eyebrows. I gave myself Adam. Adam was always separate from his group, even when he was a part of it. Shorter than the others, he always stuck out above them. That was when he began to think that maybe his preparation for his bar mitzvah was futile, because a week at the camp felt like a whole year, so by early March he felt he was already twenty-five, maybe a little younger, he wasn't quite sure of his calculations, but certainly older than he really was, so the bar mitzvah ritual was moot. He had earned his maturity during his second week there, when he turned fifteen, if we use his method of calculation, when he first bent over a person who had died. More precisely, an old woman who had died. Whether or not he got closer to God at that moment is tough to say. Maybe he merely saw that the path leading to God had far more turns in it than the image he had carried within himself. Here it looked like a winding path along a sunny slope, not very steep, so that climbing up would require almost no effort. All that changed when he bent over the old, dead woman, when it took so much effort to straighten up that his thighs wobbled and his knees buckled. In an ancient book it is written, I said, that sometimes you have to lean way down in order to see the face of the Lord. And now picture, each of you in your own mind, I went on, the faces of the people whose names you've been given. And not only their names, imagine them as whole people, their every move, every part of their body, each of you be the person, feel how that person's muscles tense and their lungs fill, dream their dreams, okay, no one was dreaming there, so instead just look, look with their eyes, and wait in a way you have never waited. Götz and Meyer would probably have been confused by such volubility, hardly surprising if you keep in mind the conciseness of military language and its resistance to gushing feeling. The students were also confused: what sort of waiting did I have in mind? Waiting, I said, for something to happen that would finally make some sense, because it was simply not possible that all this could be happening without making any sense. Then the waiting, I said, took the shape of a rumor about being transferred to a camp in Romania or maybe Poland, to a safer place, somewhere settled, the story had it, with other Jews and far enough from that city on the other shore, which was closing its eyes shamelessly to the scenes of their precipitous fall. While all this was going on, Götz and Meyer were receiving instructions for their special assignment, then they devoted themselves to checking even the most minute technical details of their Saurer's special equipment. All that was left was to depart, which they soon did, heading toward people who, though at first glance seemingly motionless, were actually hurtling toward the two of them, waiting for them on precisely the spot where we are now standing. Then I began a roll call, to turn them into little family groups, to arrange them in a column, and, though a little disorderly, they marched with even steps to the gate to the Fairgrounds camp. The bus was waiting, bathed in sunlight. The driver was asleep, resting his cheek on his arms folded over the steering wheel. As I called their names and as they got onto the bus, I told them they should imagine how the person whose name they carried entered the gray truck, whose dimensions I had repeated several times and which was driven by Götz and Meyer. You can't see them now, I said, but take my word for it, they were refined gentlemen. Götz, or maybe Meyer, one of them, wouldn't, as people often say, harm a fly, but he was capable of tossing a cat from the roof down into the concrete yard. Cats are stupid, he said, I would never like to be a cat. No one laughed. Adam turned and glared at me. I started to say the names, the bus filled slowly, the driver woke up, smacked his lips, and immediately began to whistle, the students' faces were grim, anxious, they were all silent, although the mothers touched the children, the husbands leaned over their wives, but all in silence, as if under water or at a very high altitude, in rarefied mountain air. Wherever it was, I found myself among my relatives, and I have no words to describe the sweetness I felt, that same way I felt when I hung the drawing of the family tree on the wall for the first time. Later I took it down, but now I am no longer certain where it is, on the wall or in a file. Perhaps that doesn't really matter. More important is what happened with Adam when he saw the gray truck. That same moment he began to understand the language spoken by Commander Andorfer and the other soldiers, suddenly he could see that there were parallel worlds, that the worlds were created by language, and that it was enough to alter the meaning of several words in order to change the existing world into a new one. And he saw precisely where that new camp was, the one about which Commander Andorfer had informed the members of the Administration did, indeed, exist, and what route one had to take to get there. He didn't know precisely what went on inside the gray truck, because he was not familiar with how an automobile engine works. He had never been interested in such things. Then one night he dreamed that from the dense darkness, faces of people who were asphyxiating flew out before him. He opened his eyes and stared at the pale darkness of the great hall, filled with all the possible sounds the human body can produce. So it was that he was awake and saw the moment when the hall would be empty, and he almost fainted at the deafening silence. But before that, I said into the microphone, we must see, no, we can't see, because the people whose names you carry were in the dark, we must feel what they felt, packed into the Saurer, driven by Götz and Meyer. At first there wasn't much, I mean, they felt almost nothing, they just groped in the dark for their nearest of kin, and they spoke, they all spoke at the same time, so that Adam, although far from them, heard quite clearly how the spoken words were smashing and shattering. The truck stopped two or three times, but it started up again soon, and then someone recognized by the sound that they were crossing the bridge. They were going back, at last, to Belgrade. Then just when they began to try and guess which streets they were driving along, the truck stopped. The people whose names you bear fell silent, I said, and then they listened tensely in the dark. They heard voices, recognized German, but none of them understood the words, then the door slammed, someone walked along the truck, went back, stood, you heard some sort of rattling on the floor, and as if that had been some predetermined signal, everyone began to speak at once, to shout and bang the sides of the truck, until the door to the cab slammed again and the engine started up. Adam claimed that at that point you could hear birds, but I don't know whether he can be believed. The truck, apparently, was driving through town, and it would have to go quite far before they would be anywhere near a wood with birds. Götz and Meyer also don't remember any birds, though sometimes, if I am not mistaken, they told it differently. Whatever the case, soon after that second start, the people whose names you bear began to notice the smell of fuel exhaust. At first it was pleasant, like some secret bond with the outside world, and then more and more repellent, but sweetish, followed by nausea, a powerful headache, choking, hoarse screams, although there were those who lowered their heads and fell asleep. I touched my lips to the head on the microphone and looked at the students. Most of them were straining to breathe, one girl had clutched her throat, someone's hand struggled feebly toward the window and then slid helplessly back, one boy covered his eyes with his hands, two girls had their arms round each other, their heads on one another's shoulders, I saw some lips moving, but except for the driver's soft whistling I heard no sounds. If we keep this up, Adam thought, all of us are going to die. He went over to the carpenter's workshop and asked if they had anything he could use to poke holes in an aluminum partition. How thick? asked the carpenter. Adam showed a thickness between his index finger and his thumb: This thick, he said. You are not big enough to manage a drill, answered the carpenter, but you could handle a spike and bang it through with a hammer. A spike, a drill, a rasp, it didn't matter, the carpenter was right, Adam wasn't up to handling tools, he wouldn't be able to use them, with the best of will he couldn't have done because Adam was weak, he had no strength in his arms, no force to his swing. He had to come up with something else. But what was happening to you, I asked, here? No one answered. One student's tongue protruded from his lips. Most of them were sitting, eyes closed, though there were some who were staring, motionless, but all of them had faces twisted, convulsed, in revulsion or pain. We can only guess, I said, what they felt as their knees gradually gave way, as they slipped to the floor, pressed down by the other bodies, pushed by hands that were clutching at whatever they touched, some were still shouting, showing not the slightest inclination to let up, and then suddenly the dark began to disperse, and in that bright light they could no longer see anything. I put down the microphone and went down the aisle. I opened several windows, patted the young man on the cheek whose tongue was protruding from his lips, pulled back the curtain the dark-haired girl had used to hide her face. Using the route we are using now, I said, or one very much like it, but certainly in Götz and Meyer's truck, about five thousand people passed right through the center of town over the next few weeks. Their names were different, but they were always the same people, just as they were this time. Boringly similar, Götz, or Meyer, on whom Belgrade hadn't left much of an impression, would have said. Götz, or was it Meyer, did enjoy a lovely sunset one evening while he was strolling about the Kalemegdan fortress, though later on, when he thought back, he associated that image with a place in Ukraine where another river flowed, and there was a camp there, too, and all in all, a soldier's life is monotonous, no two ways about it, it is possible to make a mistake, no one loses or gains anything. I stopped talking and sat down in the last, empty row. I admit I no longer knew what to say. The bus drove through Karadjordje Park and descended toward the Autokomanda part of town. It was somewhere here, I said, that this same kind of silence reigned in that gray truck. The only people speaking were Götz and Meyer, but they were up in the cab, debating about a black cat because of which Götz, or maybe Meyer, the one who was driving, had to brake. Though maybe, since traffic was not as bad then as it is now, maybe the souls were still parting from the limp bodies and rising toward the corner, where they were awaited by the shining of the other souls, the light that the dying had discerned in the dark. Although the carbon monoxide could no longer hurt them, they still breathed a sigh of relief when they reached the end of their trip, in Jajinci, and through the open door wafted out into the fresh air, up to the heights. The souls couldn't know that this was Jajinci, I said, just as you don't know that, the place doesn't exist for you, it exists only for me, and it existed, of course, for Götz and Meyer, although they tried to speak of it as seldom as possible, because they could never pronounce it correctly. In their jargon, Jajinci was "that place." For example: We are driving a load to "that place" again. Meanwhile Adam has been frantically trying to catch up with time. He was certain poison was being introduced into the truck. He couldn't figure out how, but those faces from his dream convinced him he wasn't mistaken. Everything is true, even what we dream. No, I said, Adam didn't know this was Jajinci, haven't I explained that already? I got up again and walked to the front of the bus. The driver was whistling pretty loudly now, mumbling two or three words now and then, something like a refrain. I picked up the microphone, coughed, and then I turned, faced the students who had sunk into other people's bodies. I spoke to them like a hypnotist who has to wake his audience. He walks among the rows before that moment, removing what he wants from their pockets and their hearts, convinced all the while that they are somewhere, in other worlds from which they will return borne by rapture, unable to notice immediately what has been taken. But what happens, I find myself wondering, if the hypnotist makes a mistake somewhere, those worlds are easy to create but difficult to sustain, and it would be easy for there to be collisions, overlap, balancing of coordinates, and what if, halfway through, so to speak, someone wanders from one and crosses over to another? I mean if the hypnotist says something and claps his hands, which world will the people who have been hypnotized wake up in? I would like your attention, I said. I did not clap my hands, but they all listened: they moved their dulled, and then clearer and clearer, eyes in my direction, they straightened up in their seats, smoothed their hair, moistened their lips. Over the next fifty days, I said, Götz and Meyer's truck traveled this same route once, or sometimes twice, a day, except Sundays. Sunday is the day of rest. Every Sunday Götz and Meyer went for a walk, played cards, drank beer. Every Monday, however, they arrived promptly at the gate to the camp, tidy, shaved, they didn't even have bloodshot eyes. Unlike Adam's bloodshot eyes, a consequence, he reckoned, of his sleepless nights spent concocting a plan to master whatever it was that was suffocating the people in the back of the gray truck. By this time we had got to Jajinci, and here, without allowing them a chance to even breathe in the fresh air, started the long story about how the work was organized, how they dug the graves and buried the corpses, I mentioned the five Serbian prisoners, of whom there may have been seven, and then skipped forward two years and talked about how they burned the corpses on this very same site, about sifting through the ashes for valuables, and how, according to witness statements, the ash was dumped into the Sava River somewhere on Čukarica, where fishermen later found coins, belt buckles, buttons, wallets, metal lapel pins. I couldn't stop, despite the pleading looks of my students and their sickened grimaces. Then the driver said it was high time for us to be getting back. But we mustn't forget Adam, who had finally worked out that what he had been thinking about so much was close at hand. Naturally: a gas mask. Easy to think of, impossible to do, another way of saying the same thing. But if there can be such a place as this camp, Adam wondered, then why shouldn't everything be possible, and why shouldn't it be possible that there might be a boy at the camp who finds a way to get hold of one simple gas mask? The first reality is already so unreal that nothing within it seems unreal anymore, Adam might have thought, but instead, he immediately latched onto the practical details, trying to answer the questions: "where" and "when," because everything depended on them, especially that slender thread that keeps life going, and to which every "why" is a weight that threatens to interrupt it. In short: he remembered that at the camp headquarters building, where he sometimes went to do one little job or another, right by the entrance, on a shelf, he had spotted several gas masks, left there, as far as he could tell, for the officers working in that place. All he had to do was find the right moment, a time when he could grab one of them, and the best time seemed when a new transport was being prepared, and when most of the officers and soldiers were busy keeping order. So it was. Don't ask me how it happened, perhaps Adam was invisible that day, but while the women and children were climbing up into the gray truck, Adam strode, the gas mask under his shirt, toward a secret place where he would hide the mask until the day when his turn came. I know this is going on too long, but there are some things you can't describe differently. I hope that the driver will understand, I said, and all of them, as if by command, looked at the driver, who first turned round, as if there were someone standing behind him, and then shrugged helplessly. And so it was, when the moment came, that Adam tucked the gas mask under his shirt, put on his thick sweater and winter coat, hunched over to cover the bulge over his stomach, and took his little suitcase to the other truck, the one that came into the camp, and then went over to the gate, where they were gathering the group set for transport. Not far from them, one of the drivers was giving the children candy. Which means, I said, that now we can go back to the bus. Adam was among the first to get on and made his way to the farthest corner. He looked around but could hardly see a thing, because the truck quickly filled with people who were pushing and pressing against each other, trying to find as comfortable a spot as possible for the long journey. Then the door began to close, and most of them turned toward it, which meant that Adam had a little more room, using it to slip out of his coat. In the meantime, people were calling to each other in the dark, women were summoning their children, children were crying, someone cursed angrily, a voice, suddenly and clearly, said: What matters is that we're leaving, and everyone fell silent. Adam sniffed carefully, but all he could sense were the smells of human bodies. Maybe there is no poison, he thought, maybe they will just drive us around until we suffocate from lack of air. But all his doubts were dispersed when the truck stopped altogether, the engine died, and everything got quiet, and you could hear someone's footsteps, then a rattling that seemed to come through under their feet. Adam unbuttoned his shirt. Who knows how, in the dark, when the truck started up again and you could smell the fumes in the air, he managed with all the bands and buckles, but he pulled the mask over his face, and after two or three trial breaths, he started breathing evenly. Everything that followed he already knew from his dream, but still, despite the dark, he closed his eyes. He opened them only when all sound had died away in the truck, and he clearly heard someone in the cab repeat, in German: *Es ist aus, es ist aus*. He tried to push away the body pressing against his legs, but it kept coming back and got heavier and heavier, so that in the end, when the truck stopped and the door started opening, he barely managed to maneuver out of his corner. The door had swung open by then, light was streaming into the smoke-filled truck, and Adam saw how the tangled heap of people was moving as if alive, and at the same time, stumbling, as if hurtling toward the source of light. Then this subsided, you could hear voices outside, and Adam slowly followed the smoke that was spilling out of the truck. He made his way with difficulty, climbing over the heaped-up bodies. When he peeked out, first he saw the sky, then greenery and excavated earth, all of it through a haze, and then he met the gaze of a man in a white shirt. Adam raised his hand to wipe the glass on the mask, and the man stumbled, fell to his knees, and began to cross himself. It took Adam a little time to fiddle with the bands and buckles, then he slid down the tangled bodies closer to the door, and here he proceeded to remove the mask. Somehow this part was harder than putting it on, so that he didn't even notice when the man in the white shirt was approached by a German soldier who smacked him on the back with his rifle butt. When Adam finally saw the soldier, he was raising his gun toward Adam, and Adam realized he could see him quite clearly, no trace of fog, he could even see the fine lines around the man's eyes, squinting a little in the sun. How interesting, thought Adam, who was a curious boy, how does the bullet propel from the barrel? Then, slowly, the soldier's trigger finger whitened with pressure. Adam didn't hear the shot, but Commander Andorfer who, with Scharführer Götz, or possibly Meyer, was having a cigarette across the field, heard it. What was that? Commander Andorfer asked, his right hand in his pocket. Sounds as if someone fired a shot. He dipped his hand into the pocket, pulled out the little bag of cough drops and offered them to the Scharführer. They listened, listened, but heard nothing. During that time Adam was falling. He fell slowly, bit by bit, as if crumbling, as if, he thought, he'd never fall all the way, but once he was almost to the ground, he felt how he suddenly pulled free of himself and rose slowly, straight up, skyward, until the people on the ground were tiny ants. So, said the driver, should we go back to the school? If I hadn't been holding the microphone, I would have fallen, his voice shocked me so. I did muster the strength to say yes, and I caught sight of a little flicker in the glassy eyes of my students. For homework, I said, and the flicker was instantly snuffed out, write a composition on the theme: "Today I Am Someone Else." I put the microphone back in its place, turned off the sound system. Adam was dead. I'd thought, I'd hoped he would survive. I could have lain down between the bus seats and fallen asleep instantly, I was so drained. It isn't easy to show someone that the world, like a sock, has its other side, and that all you need is one skillful twist to switch one side to the other, skillful and quick, so that no one notices the change, but everyone accepts that the wrong side is in fact the right side of the world. The bus stopped and the students rushed off, mumbling their good-byes. The driver took out the papers I had to sign, and for a moment, while I scribbled the letters that comprised my name, I thought of asking him how he had understood the story about the inside-out world, but then I noticed his lips, pursed, ready to whistle, and I gave up. There was something in that mouth that reminded me of Götz's and Meyer's lips, though I'd never seen them and could only imagine them, but I really did imagine them that way, at least in part, at least at the moment when Götz, or Meyer, raised his razor and started shaving. In all this the lips have no meaning whatsoever, I don't know why I mention them. When I got off the bus, three of the girls from the class came over. They all three spoke at once, and, as far as I could gather, they wanted to know whether I truly believe that people have souls. I do believe that, I said. But Adam, the highest treble among the girls asked, was he greeted, I mean was his soul met by someone up there? We stared up at the sky for a moment. Of course, I said, they were all up there, a whole throng of golden souls hovering nearby, he could feel how all the pain poured from him and vanished into the endless blue. Yes, yes, yes, they said, again all three of them with one breath, obviously impatient, but in that case, they immediately wanted to know, if souls already exist, can they be lost? Of course they can, I said, although a soul that remembers can never be lost. Don't all souls remember? they asked, surprised. Some of them don't, I said, some try to forget. Yes, yes, yes, they said, thanked me, turned away, and left. That was all I needed: a riddle at the end of a day full of dying. Today I had already been Adam, Commander Andorfer, Götz and Meyer, the Serbian prisoner, and the German soldier, I could not also be an interpreter of human souls, regardless of the fact that I speak of them as if I meet them daily. I have never seen a soul, and I can only imagine one, just as I picture Götz and Meyer, whom I have also never seen. I did, indeed, one night, starting suddenly from a dream, catch sight beneath the ceiling of a small, silvery body, round and completely transparent, and when I blinked, it vanished. Now I am prepared to believe that that was a soul, perhaps not mine, but nevertheless a soul, although at the time I convinced myself that it was the afterglow of the headlights from a car that had rushed by in the road. In short, the talk of the soul reminded me that I had recently, maybe two weeks before, contemplated suicide. It was a moment when I asked myself for the umpteenth time, as I leafed through documents from the file of witness statements, what I would have done had I been at the camp and understood at one point, as the prisoners surely must ultimately have understood, that the transports in the gray truck were not the beginning of a journey to the promised camp, in Romania or Poland, but rather that in there, in the truck, hid the beginning and end of every journey – would I have waited obediently, even then, for the inevitable spin of the wheel of fate, or would I have sought some way to circumvent it? It was evening, I was already exhausted, and something else was demanding my attention, so that only later, as I was brushing my teeth, did it occur to me: I'd kill myself. Once that idea had nudged my consciousness, I could no longer shake it off. I lay there in bed, in the dark, breathing deeply and waiting for my heart to stop pounding. My resolve shocked me, there is no point in pretending it didn't, despite the fact that it was expressed in the conditional tense. It didn't take me long to get from there to the present time, not, of course, grammatical, but real, time, the one enveloping us. Here I should mention that I had earlier thought of suicide as an act of cowardice and was truly surprised by my readiness to see in it something else, for instance: the right to the choice of one's last minute in life. I was drawn to the possibility of interpreting that as a symbolic liberation from Götz and Meyer, a statement of my superiority and their defeat. Taking everything into consideration, the most natural way to do it, if you can say such a thing of suicide, would be ending my life in a car. All I had to do was find an empty place, attach the exhaust pipe to a rubber hose and run the other end into the car, turn on the engine, close my eyes and wait. I ignored the fact that I had no car and did not know how to drive, but for that reason I spent a great deal of time debating the music for my funeral: first I thought of Mozart, anything of Mozart's, I'd always enjoyed his lightness, then I remembered Villa-Lobos and his compositions for the guitar, and finally I decided I would be more radical, but I couldn't make up my mind between Stockhausen and Cage. I don't know whether all people contemplating suicide are so finicky, but a long time spent going through my records convinced me that I had been mistaken and that I'd never have the strength to turn against myself, not the courage or the cowardice, not in a camp or outside it, rather I'd wait, like most people, for fate to come for me. I hesitated regarding Götz and Meyer, and real death seemed too high a price for a symbolic victory. So the rubber tube, which I had bought, just in case, in the market, is still in the bathroom, next to the tub. There, everything comes down to the same choice between victory and defeat. There is no middle road. If I had been in my flat at that moment, I wouldn't have missed the chance to write that on a piece of paper and put it in the file with my name on it: there is no middle road. Aside from memory, of course, as I explained to my students: a soul that remembers cannot be lost. I know that I have already said that and that I'm repeating myself, but it is not my fault that life is built on repetitions and that its movement, which resembles a straight line, actually goes round in circles. We are like a dog chasing its tail but never catching it. There, I'm talking about dogs, and not the little fish in the aquarium that I did not manage to keep alive. One by one they flipped over on their backs and stared at me, balefully, with their rigid eyes. So it goes: first the fish are betrayed, then everyone else. My relatives, for instance. Then, in the grocer's window, I caught sight of my reflection among the vegetables and biscuits and thought that I was being unfair toward that hunched, balding man. Everyone could see how much effort it took him to bear the burden of his years, though at least I knew that it was the weight of memory, the capacity of memory, that was at issue. Luckily I was close to home just then, and I could catch my breath. First I leaned against a signpost, then I wanted to sit on the bonnet of a parked car, but its alarm went off and I had to walk away quickly, turning back frequently, as if I, the innocent passerby, just happened to be interested in what was happening. I went into my apartment, out of breath, and sat for a long time in the front hall, on the floor, undoing my shoelaces. I got up, avoiding the mirror on the opposite wall. Today I had already been so many people that I was afraid of what I'd see there. With my head bowed, my eyes closed, I slipped into my slippers and went into the kitchen. The bottle of homemade brandy and three glasses were still on the table, a trace of Götz and Meyer's unexpected visit a few nights back. I don't know why I'd never put them away, but I remembered the order of the glasses: mine stood a little farther away from the other two, closer to the bottle, which it nearly touched with its wide rim. I drew the glass to me, then the bottle, and poured myself a brandy, just a little, only enough for me to lick it and taste how it burned. Sometimes all we need is the burning, I have to say that, regardless of the fact that I'm not one of those people familiar with rage. If I were, who knows how my encounter with Götz and Meyer would have ended on that bench at the old people's home in the foothills of the Alps. It is good that they are not here. The burning might push a person to do things he might later regret. And so, without letting go of the glass, I went into the sitting room. I call it the sitting room, though generally I lie on the sofa in the evenings.

There are times I sit there, too, until late at night. In the silence, behind one of the walls, you can hear the cuckoo in a wall clock. I switched on the light. There were no traces of any kind, not even mine. I no longer wondered where the drawing of my family tree was: it was on the wall, as it used to be. I stood there in front of it and carefully read each name, the years of birth and death, and the question marks. When I started, I believed that by working out what was behind the question marks I would resolve the meaning of the question mark I had become, but I hadn't even got as far as the dot under it. I brought my glass to my nose: it smelled of brandy but without the burning, if burning has a smell. I looked over again at the sketch of the family tree with its cropped treetop out of which a few, nearly dry, branches protruded. It was easy to see that this tree would no longer bear fruit, you didn't need to be especially clever to realize that, just as those people who cropped it didn't need to be much good at gardening. Götz and Meyer, for instance, though it wouldn't have surprised me had I learned that one of them tended roses. Then it seemed to me that I heard a noise from the kitchen, but first I wanted to be sure that the sketch of the family tree understood what I had done today: that I, in picturesque terms, had sowed the seeds of remembering among my students, especially among those three girls from the class; there would be no fruit from that seed, but if it fell on fertile ground, at least that would prevent the weeds of forgetting from growing. Because as long as there is remembering, that was what I had really wanted to say to them, there is a chance, no matter how slim, that someone, once, somewhere, will look at the real faces of Götz and Meyer, something I hadn't managed to do. And as long as their faces are nothing but a stand-in for any face, Götz and Meyer will return and repeat the meaninglessness of history that becomes, in the end, the meaninglessness of our lives. The tree is silent, it does not answer. I, too, say nothing. After a few words there is no longer any point in speaking. Sounds come from the kitchen again, and I turn, still holding the glass, and walk toward the kitchen door. There is no one, however, in the kitchen. Two glasses, rinsed, are upside down on the edge of the sink. On the table, right in the middle, is the coiled rubber tubing. Next to the tubing is a piece of paper, and on it lies a pencil, though there is nothing on the paper. There is no bottle, but now I have no time to look for it. I put down the glass, walk into the front hall and listen. It turns out that I am listening in the wrong direction, because the noise that finds me, no louder than the rustling of papers, comes from my left, from behind the door of the study. I go over there slowly, on tiptoe, my calves and thighs ache with the effort. As I walk, I reach for a weapon, any weapon, because I know, I know who is behind that door and what they are doing, although I have never seen them and can only imagine them. I catch sight of the umbrella hanging on the coat stand, old-fashioned, all of a piece, with a long ferrule and curved bamboo handle. I take it, tuck the handle under my right arm, nudge the door open, and with the umbrella brandished like a spear, I burst into the study with a shriek. The point needn't even be sharp, I think, as I lunge through the dark. I feel slowed by resistance, the shudder of penetration, then lurch, full force, into the wall.

Author's Note

The historical facts on which this story is based come from numerous sources – archival material, encyclopedia entries, newspaper articles, books, and studies – but the most important source was Milan Koljanin's monograph on the German Camp at the Belgrade Fairgrounds, published by Institut za savremenu istoriju, Belgrade, 1992, and the study by Christopher Browning, "The final solution in Serbia: The Judenlager at the Fairgrounds," published in Serbian translation in *Zbornik 6*, SJOJ, Belgrade, 1992. A story, however, is never history, and it respects the facts only insofar as those facts suit the story.

I owe a special debt of gratitude to Milica Mihailović, curator at the Jewish Historical Museum in Belgrade, who kindly searched for answers to all my questions. Her suggestions were always valuable.

I am also grateful to the Levin Smolar Foundation, whose grant allowed me to work without interruption or hindrance.